Julie raised her hand to cover the scar. 'I am happy with my face the way it is,' she said stiffly.

Pierre reached out and, taking her hand, gently pulled it away. 'It *is* a beautiful face,' he said, looking her directly in the eyes.

He was so close she could almost distinguish the individual eyelashes framing his deep blue eyes. Eyelashes like that were wasted on a man, she thought, trying to ignore the way her heart had started galloping. Then what he had said sank in. He had called her beautiful. Her heart beat even faster. Did he really believe that? She gave herself a mental shake. No, of course he didn't—he was just being kind. It was far more likely that he just couldn't stop himself from complimenting every woman who crossed his path.

'Your bone structure is perfect,' he continued, scrutinising her face with a professional eye. 'You are lucky. No amount of plastic surgery can ever improve on that.'

Anne Fraser was born in Scotland, but brought up in South Africa. After she left school she returned to the birthplace of her parents, the remote Western Islands of Scotland. She left there to train as a nurse, before going on to university to study English Literature. After the birth of her first child, she and her doctor husband travelled the world, working in rural Africa, Australia and Northern Canada. Anne still works in the health sector. To relax, she enjoys spending time with her family, reading, walking and travelling.

Recent titles by the same author:

POSH DOC CLAIMS HIS BRIDE
HER VERY SPECIAL BOSS
DR CAMPBELL'S SECRET SON

FALLING FOR HER MEDITERRANEAN BOSS

BY
ANNE FRASER

MILLS & BOON™
Pure reading pleasure™

All the characters in this book have no existence outside the imagination of the author, and have no relation whatsoever to anyone bearing the same name or names. They are not even distantly inspired by any individual known or unknown to the author, and all the incidents are pure invention.

First published in Great Britain 2009
Harlequin Mills & Boon Limited,
Eton House, 18-24 Paradise Road, Richmond, Surrey TW9 1SR

© Anne Fraser 2009

ISBN: 978 0 263 86852 4

Set in Times Roman 10½ on 12¾ pt
03-0609-53559

Printed and bound in Spain
by Litografia Rosés, S.A., Barcelona

FALLING FOR HER MEDITERRANEAN BOSS

*Gu mo theaghlach an Uibhist—
gu h-araid Lachie—tapadh leibh.*

*(To my family in Uist—especially Lachie—
thank you.)*

CHAPTER ONE

DR JULIE MCKENZIE wrapped her fingers gratefully around her coffee-cup and sank back in her chair in the doctors' mess and closed her eyes briefly. What she wouldn't do for a couple of hours' sleep. She had been up all night. Just as she had been about to go home and crawl into bed for a couple of hours of much-needed sleep, the head of surgery—Mr Crawford— had asked her to stay on.

'The new locum consultant is starting today,' he had told Julie. 'And since you'll be working under him for your rotation on Plastics, I think it's a good idea if you stay on and meet him.'

His tone had made it clear that it wasn't optional. Besides, Julie was curious, even a little anxious, to meet her new boss. She had enjoyed working with Mr Crawford for the last six months in General Surgery, but as part of her training she was scheduled to spend the next three months attached to Plastic Surgery.

She lifted a hand and touched the scar that ran from the corner of her eye to her jawbone, feeling its raised surface under her fingertips. It was ironic, really, her working in Plastic Surgery. On the other hand, her own disfigurement meant she was drawn to the specialty. At least she would have no difficulty empathising with patients who sought help.

A polite cough aroused her from her reverie. Grief! She realised she had been on the point of dropping off. She jumped to her feet, knocking over her half-drunk cup of coffee. A hand shot out, catching the mug just in time to prevent the hot liquid from spilling over the carpet. In front of her stood Mr Crawford and, holding the errant mug, a blue-eyed man with thick black wavy hair, who was looking at her a half-smile playing on his lips.

Her heart gave an odd erratic beat. He was, by far, the most gorgeous man Julie had ever seen outside the movies. He was tall, a couple of inches over six feet at least, with eyes that glinted like diamonds. Only a slightly hooked nose prevented high cheekbones and a sensuous mouth from looking feminine in their beauty. He was lean but well built, his theatre greens sat low on narrow hips. Julie felt her mouth go dry. She couldn't ever remember having such an immediate and powerful attraction to a man before. Julie swallowed a groan. She was acutely conscious that her scrubs were crumpled and that she looked a mess after having been on her feet for twelve hours straight.

'Dr McKenzie, I'd like to introduce you to Dr Pierre Favatier, our new consultant plastic surgeon. He will be with us for the next couple of months.'

Dazed, Julie held out her hand and felt it engulfed. She looked down. He really did have the most beautiful hands, she thought, the long elegant fingers of a piano player or a surgeon.

'So this is Dr McKenzie,' he said in a deep husky voice that made her think of late nights in smoky bars.

'I'm pleased to meet you,' Julie said, mortifyingly aware that she sounded breathless.

'And I am pleased to meet you too,' he said formally echoing her greeting, and then added, 'I hope you hold a scalpel more firmly than a coffee-cup.'

She could detect a glint of humour in his eyes. God, was he aware of the effect he was having on her?

'Of course. You startled me—that's all!' she said defensively.

'Well, that's a relief,' he said politely, and, despite the gleam in his eye, Julie wasn't sure whether he was joking.

'I understand that you will be my junior while I am here? Mr Crawford speaks well of you.' He was French. That much was clear from his accent, although it was faint and only evident in the way he pronounced the h's at the beginning of words.

'Mr Crawford is right.' She cast a grateful look at her chief. 'I am an excellent surgeon—whatever first impression I gave you there.' Well, she was. In whatever other area she lacked confidence, it wasn't in her surgical ability, and although she knew she ran the risk of appearing arrogant, she wanted this man to know that she was good at what she did.

He laughed, the sound low and genuine. 'Ah, confidence. I like that in a doctor. Especially one who works with me.' His eyes narrowed. 'I do not like incompetent doctors. I have no time for them. They can learn with somebody else. I demand perfection. Are you perfect, Dr Mackenzie?' Once again there was a challenge in his ice-blue eyes, although a hint of laughter still lurked in their depths. She had the uneasy feeling he wasn't just referring to her surgical skills.

Julie squared her shoulders and eyed him coolly, striving to get her racing pulse under control. 'I don't think anybody is perfect—least of all me.' She forced a smile. 'Although, in my work, I do try.'

For a moment as their eyes locked, it was as if there was no one else in the room. His gaze dropped to her mouth then flickered feather-like over the contours of her face, before coming back to her eyes. Now she knew what animals felt when pinned by the stare of a predator. As heat flooded her cheeks, she couldn't prevent herself from raising her hand to her scar. Damn it! She hadn't meant to do that. He tilted his head and regarded her intently, speculation darkening his eyes. Her heart continued to beat as if she had just completed a downhill race.

Mr Crawford broke into the silence that seemed to crackle across the room.

'I wouldn't be allocating Julie to your team if I didn't think she was one of the best, if not the best, junior we have on the rotation at the moment,' he said mildly. 'You know, she was once a champion skier,' he added proudly, as if taking personal responsibility for Julie's successes. 'She's driven to excel in everything she does. No one works harder. She's always here at the hospital, and even when she's off duty I find her in the library at all hours, reading up on cases. So, as I said before, Dr Favatier, you can rest assured you have the best working with you.'

Julie felt her blush deepen at the praise. She hadn't been aware until now that Mr Crawford held her in such high regard. Perhaps finally all the extra effort she put in was paying off. Of course, Mr Crawford wasn't to know that a barren social life left plenty of time for work and study. She sneaked a glance at the new consultant. Despite his smile, his forehead was knotted again.

He shook his head as if to clear whatever was puzzling him. *'Bon!'* he said. 'Then I am satisfied. Too many young doctors have other distractions.'

Julie's eyebrows rose. With his dark good looks and blatant sex appeal, he struck her as a man who would enjoy many 'distractions', as he so oddly put it. Catching her look, Pierre winked at her. The gesture was so unexpected Julie thought she must have imagined it. He was her boss after all! Nevertheless, she felt her blush extend to the tips of her ears and wished she had managed to find the time to shower and change before Mr Crawford had waylaid her. But, she told herself impatiently, what did it matter what Dr Favatier thought of her appearance? Someone who looked the way he did was hardly the type of man to look twice at her—even if she was dressed up to the nines. Nevertheless, she had to fight against the impulse to release her hair from its ponytail and let it fall across her face and cover the scar.

Dr Crawford turned to Julie. 'And you are extremely fortunate to have the chance to work with Dr Favatier. He's considered a pioneer in reconstructive plastic surgery in his own country. We are very lucky to have him here for the next couple of months so we must—and I know you will—make the most of the time we have with him to learn as much as possible.'

'Of course,' Julie replied, thinking frantically of all the extra reading she'd have squeeze in to make sure she was up to speed. 'Thank you, Mr Crawford. And I'm very pleased to have the opportunity to work with you, Dr Favatier.'

'C'mon, then Pierre, let's leave Dr McKenzie to get herself home for some well-deserved rest. There's a case in Theatre I'd like your opinion on.' Pierre gave Julie one last searching look, before allowing Mr Crawford to usher him out the door.

'Get some rest, Julie, and we'll see you soon,' her chief said over his shoulder.

Once the two men had gone, Julie sank back in her chair.

For some unfathomable reason she felt as if she had just been caught up in the middle of a tornado. A tornado that had only subsided when her new boss had left the room. He was a hunk. There was no denying it. But, Julie reminded herself with an inward grimace that hunks had no place in her life or, more to the point, she in theirs. Just as well, then, that the only thing that mattered to her was whether he would be a good teacher. And from Dr Crawford's introduction, it seemed there was plenty to be learned from Dr Pierre Favatier.

Julie let the beat take over as she relaxed into the rhythm of the music from the DJ. She liked the way the darkness of the club hid her. For once, she felt totally unselfconscious. She rarely ventured out in the evening unless Kim, her best and only friend, persuaded her, but tonight, as a special favour to Richard, she had agreed to come to his eighteenth birthday celebration at the nightclub.

'You don't want me there,' she had protested earlier in the week when he had asked her. 'I'm too old—I'll only spoil the evening for you.'

But he had insisted. 'Please, Julie. My friends will think it's really cool to have you there—you once being famous and all. And, besides, you're not old—not really.'

Julie had to laugh, knowing that at twenty-six she probably did seem old to Richard and his friends, plus she'd never really been *famous*. Eventually she had given in and agreed to go, knowing that tonight was especially important to him. She had met Richard at St Margaret's hospice, where her mother had spent the last few weeks of her life, and had got to know the young lad with the friendly and cheerful personality well. Richard had been suffering from a childhood form of leukaemia, and before he had become ill had liked to ski, and on the occasions he'd felt well enough he'd persuaded Julie to take him to the dry ski slopes on the outskirts of town.

Recently he and his family had been given the news they had so desperately being praying for. Richard's disease was in remission, and tonight was a special celebration of his recovery, as well as a birthday party.

As Julie danced with her young protégé, she had the uncomfortable feeling someone was watching her. Raising her eyes she was disconcerted to see Dr Pierre Favatier on the balcony, his gaze fixed on her. For a moment their eyes locked and Julie felt her world shift. His brow furrowed before he turned his head to scan the room as if searching for someone in the mass. What was he doing there? It was the last place she had expected to see him and she wondered who he was with. He looked out of place in his suit and tie, she thought. Hardly clubbing gear. Had he, not knowing the city too well, wandered in by accident, mistaking the club for some other, more sophisticated venue?

Julie contemplated going over to him and saying hello, but for some reason she felt shy and awkward about approaching him. Instead, when his eyes rested on hers again, she lifted a hand and gave him a small wave of recognition. She only had time to catch a glimpse of his return wave before Richard pulled her around.

'What's happening over there, Julie?' the teenager asked, gesturing with his chin to where a crowd of dancers had stopped moving to the music. People were standing on tiptoe, looking towards the rear of the club.

Then, as the music came to a sudden halt, there was a

ripple of unease in the crowd. Someone called out and necks craned to see what the fuss was about. A fire alarm sounded and the agitated voice of the DJ came over the speaker system.

'Could everybody, please, make their way to the nearest exit? Do not panic. Do not stop to collect your belongings. I repeat, could everybody make their way as quickly as possible to the fire exits?'

Now Julie could smell the faint, but distinctive smell of smoke. There was a moment's stillness, as if no one could believe what was happening, then pandemonium broke out. The crowd turned and started pushing and shoving their way to the exits, almost knocking Julie off her feet.

Julie grabbed hold of her dancing companion. 'Richard,' she said urgently, 'I want you to get out of here as fast as you can—without panicking. I'm going to see if anyone needs help.'

Frightened eyes looked at her. 'Come, too,' Richard shouted over the noise.

'I'll be all right. Trust me.' She shoved him in the direction of the nearest fire exit. 'Just go. Quickly! But don't panic,' she warned again.

She turned against the heaving tide of bodies. Her heart was pounding. More than anything she would have liked to follow Richard to safety, but she fought against the instinct to save herself. She couldn't. Not until she was sure that everyone was out of the building.

The lights flickered, dimmed and then went out completely. In the sudden darkness, fear turned to terror and the throng surged forward with more determination than ever. Cries of alarm drowned the voice of the DJ pleading for calm. Even when the emergency lighting came on, Julie knew his entreaties were too late. There was widespread panic now as people were pushed to the floor and trampled by fellow clubbers in their driving need to get to the exits. Julie knelt beside a young girl who had fallen in the crush. Julie had to fight hard to stay upright as still more people pushed past. The girl was conscious, but in need of help.

'Are you okay?' she asked. The girl nodded, looking up at Julie with a tear-stained face. 'I think so, but someone stood on my ankle.' She sat up and clutched her right foot, clearly in pain.

Bracing herself, Julie pulled the injured clubber to her feet. 'Can you walk on it?'

The girl tried, testing her weight, but Julie had to catch her as her ankle gave way.

'Lean against me, I'll help you,' she said. Before she could begin to shuffle her towards the exit, Pierre appeared by her side. Julie had never been so glad to see anyone in her life.

'I'll take her,' he shouted in her ear. 'Follow me.' Then he scooped the frightened girl into his arms and headed towards the exit. Julie watched his retreating back for a second, before turning and heading back against the flow of bodies still pushing their way out. However much every nerve in her body was telling her to get out, there was no way she could leave while there were still people inside. She had almost reached the rear of the room, where Richard's group had been sitting, when she found herself face to face with Susan, one of the youngest of Richard's friends.

'Susan, Are you all right? Why haven't you got out? Where's everyone else?'

Susan eyes darted from side to side. She looked terrified. 'They're all out, except Martha. She went to the toilet shortly before the alarm went off. I don't want to leave without her. Please, help me find her!' She clutched at Julie, her voice catching on a sob. 'She must be around here somewhere!'

'Slow down, Susan.' Julie grasped the young girl by the shoulders, forcing her to look directly into her eyes. 'Tell me where you've looked.'

'Everywhere. I don't know where she could be!' Susan coughed. The smoke was getting thicker, making it difficult to see. On the far side of the room Julie could see flames leaping towards the roof. She knew it wouldn't be long before the building was completely ablaze.

'Don't worry, I'll find her. You get out.' She shoved Susan in the direction of the exit. Then she lifted the bottom of her T-shirt and covered her mouth. It wouldn't be much protection against the smoke, but it might buy her a few minutes. Julie was relieved to hear sirens in the distance. The rescue services were on their way.

The main dancing area was almost empty, most of the revellers having made it outside. However, even in the smoke-filled atmosphere Julie could make out at least two bodies lying on the floor. For a moment she hesitated. What should she do? Continue to look for Martha, or help the victims on the floor? The fire had already spread alarmingly in the short period of time she had been talking to Susan and tongues of crimson flames were now creeping towards the bodies. There was a good chance Martha was outside and safe. But unless she did something for the collapsed victims, they would be in danger of being consumed by the fire. She couldn't afford to wait for the firefighters. Before she could act, her attention was drawn by movement towards the rear of the room. The DJ was trying desperately to beat out flames that were licking up his arms. For a moment their eyes held. Julie had never seen such abject terror before. His attempts to extinguish the flames were proving futile, and Julie could see that in the short time she had stood, horror-struck, they had spread from his arms across his chest. It was clear that unless someone did something, and quickly, the DJ would have no chance.

Realising that she had only a few seconds at the most, she rushed towards him. She had only taken a couple of steps when felt herself yanked backwards. She was swung around to face Pierre.

'I thought you were following me out!' he said, his accent more evident than ever. Even in the dim, smoke-filled light Julie could see his eyes glinting with anger.

She wrenched her arm out of his grasp.

'Let me go!' She pointed over to the DJ who had fallen to the floor. 'I need to help him!'

Pierre took in the situation at a glance. 'You get the others, I'll get him.' Before Julie had a chance to protest he was moving towards the stricken man. Whipping off his jacket, he wrapped it around the DJ and rolled him around to smother the flames.

Tearing her eyes away from the two men, Julie hurried over to the inert form of a female clubber lying on the floor. The girl was barely conscious and Julie knew she had to move her out of the reach of the fire. Blocking out the terrifying crackling of the flames, Julie put her arms under the girl's armpits and started dragging her across the floor. It was hard going. The limp body was deadweight and the smoke was beginning to make breathing almost impossible. But then, just as she thought she could go no further, firemen in their full firefighting gear appeared and relieved Julie of her burden. Gesticulating towards the exit, it was clear that they were ordering Julie out of the building.

'Help them!' She pointed to the DJ and Pierre, her eyes

streaming. Thank God, the flames that had been licking the DJ's torso appeared to be almost out. Julie was finding it difficult to speak and her chest hurt. 'And there's someone else that needs help over there.'

One of the firemen nodded and made for the other victim while another firefighter grasped her arm and propelled her out of the building. She tried to resist, not wanting to leave until she was sure Pierre and the other casualties were all right, but she was no match for the burly firefighter.

Outside, the shock of freezing night air made Julie gasp. Bending over, she rested her hands on her knees for the few moments it took for her to stop coughing and for her eyes to stop streaming. Dazed, she looked up and could barely comprehend the scene before her. It was reminiscent of footage of disasters she had seen on television. At least four fire engines lit the area in swirling patterns of red and blue. Numerous clubbers stood around, looking shocked and bewildered. Several more were sitting on the ground, struggling for breath or sobbing quietly. Snow had started to fall in large wet drops, but everyone seemed oblivious to it. As her laboured breathing normalised, Pierre swept past her, carrying the unconscious figure of the DJ in his arms. In the moving beams of light from the emergency vehicles Julie could see that the DJ was badly burnt. Pierre would need her help. She quickly checked the other victims, breathing a sigh of relief that no one appeared seriously hurt. Leaving them, she hurried over to Pierre, who had laid the DJ down on a grassy verge a safe distance from the burning building. Swallowing her horror at the extent of the injured man's burns, she dropped to her knees.

'What do you want me to do?' she asked Pierre as she searched for the DJ's carotid pulse.

Pierre glanced at her. 'Go and get yourself checked out,' he said roughly.

'I'm okay,' she fired back, shouting to make herself heard above the sounds of the sirens.

He looked at her sharply, his blue eyes drilling into hers. 'I don't have time to argue,' he said, lowering his head and beginning to breathe for his patient.

Finding what she was looking for, a faint but discernible pulse, Julie knew that they had to get some oxygen into his lungs and some fluids into his veins as quickly as possible.

'I'll get help,' she said, scrambling to her feet. 'Someone must have emergency supplies.' As she stood, an ambulance pulled up, its flashing blue lights adding to the red pulses of the fire engines, making it all seem even more surreal. *Thank God*, Julie thought. There was little she and Pierre could do for the DJ without medical equipment. Almost before the paramedics were out of the ambulance, Julie was by their side. She pointed to Pierre and the inert form of the DJ. 'Over there! They need oxygen and a drip, and any other medical equipment you might have. Stat.' The paramedics nodded and, gathering their loaded bags, rushed across to Pierre. Another couple of ambulances pulled up, their sirens cutting the cold night air, their occupants leaping out ready to offer aid.

As Julie turned back towards Pierre, Susan and Richard ran across to her.

'We've got Martha and everyone else. Are you all right?' the young girl asked, her eyes wide. Then she burst into tears.

'Hey, I'm fine.' Julie assured them, grabbing hold of Richard's arm. 'Rich, get your friends together and move them to a safe position on the other side of the road. Stay there until someone checks all of you over. Okay?'

Richard nodded and, taking the still sobbing Susan by the arm, moved away.

Julie raced over to Pierre, who was still attending to his patient. 'I'm back,' she said quietly. 'What do you want me to do?'

Pierre looked up as his patient coughed and struggled for breath. Julie took an oxygen mask from one of the paramedics and placed it over the DJ's mouth.

Pierre was looking worried. 'His throat is swelling,' he said. 'The oxygen won't get to his lungs that way.' He spoke a few words to one of the paramedics, who rushed back towards one of the ambulances. Then he turned to Julie. 'There are two main problems with someone as badly burnt as our patient. Firstly, the swelling of his throat is restricting his breathing. I'll need to do an emergency tracheostomy here—right now. If we leave it until we get him to hospital, it will be too late.' The paramedic returned and Pierre began searching through the bag she had brought. In the meantime, Julie had taken the line and drip the paramedic had passed to her earlier and found an undamaged vein in the man's groin to insert the cannula.

'The other problem is that as we resuscitate him, his skin will also start to swell, becoming like leather squeezing tighter and tighter on his chest wall. As it constricts, it squeezes down on the chest, preventing the lungs from inflating properly.' Pierre continued. 'Once I've made the hole in his throat and we're getting oxygen into his lungs, I may well have to make a few incisions into the skin on his chest.' He seemed to have found what he was looking for in the bag, and a scalpel flashed in the light. He looked straight into Julie's eyes. 'I'm going to need you to help me. You'll have to hold him steady. Can you do that? If you can't, I need to know now.'

Julie returned his look steadily. 'Just tell me what to do.'

Whatever he saw in Julie's eyes must have reassured him. He bent low over the injured man. 'I'm going to do something that will help you breathe,' he said. 'I may have to cut into your chest. It won't hurt, but I'll give you something for the pain, and then we'll get you to hospital.'

He glanced at Julie and she could tell from his expression that he didn't hold out much hope for the man on the ground. 'He won't be aware of what we're doing,' he said. Gently he tipped the man's head backwards so the front of his neck stood out and he felt below the prominence of his Adam's apple. Then swiftly, but confidently, he inserted the scalpel into the victim's trachea. Julie used a sterile swab to dab away the blood, and then Pierre inserted a tube through the incision into the throat. 'Bag him,' he instructed Julie. She fixed an ambu-bag over the tube and squeezed air into the lungs. Within seconds Julie could see the colour seeping back into the victim's face. But as Pierre had predicted, almost immediately his breathing started to become laboured again.

'*Merde!*' Pierre cursed. 'It is as I thought. He will need an emergency escharotomy—where we incise the skin on his chest to help him. I hoped the tracheostomy would be enough until we got him to hospital.' Once more he bent over the patient and, using the scalpel, scored two deep incisions across the chest. Immediately the skin parted, leaving deep furrows across the chest. To Julie the procedure seemed almost barbaric.

Pierre glanced up and, catching her questioning look, said, 'The burnt skin will have to be removed later once we are sure he is stable. He won't have felt anything even if he was conscious as the nerve endings are too badly damaged. This way he has a better chance of survival.'

'Does he?' Julie whispered. 'Does he have a chance, do you think?'

'The extent of his burns…' He shook his head. 'Well, they are bad. But I am hopeful. The sooner we get him to hospital the better. Let's get him into an ambulance.'

As the paramedics helped Julie and Pierre load the injured man onto a stretcher, Pierre said to Julie, 'I need to go with him in the ambulance.'

'I'll come with you,' she offered. 'I just need to make sure the people I'm with are okay.'

Pierre shook his head. 'We can't wait. He has to go now. Anyway, there is only room for one of us to go with him. And it is better that I go.' He hesitated, glancing over Julie's shoulder. 'Could you do something for me?'

Julie looked around. There were still four or five casualties needing medical attention but they were being attended to by paramedics. Furthermore, she could see a fluorescent jacket with 'Doctor' emblazoned on the back. It seemed as if her help here was no longer required.

'Sure,' she said. 'Just tell me what.'

'Can you drive?'

Julie was surprised at the question.

'Yes,'

'Do you have a car with you and have you been drinking?'

'No and no,' she replied.

Pierre dug around in his pocket before pulling out a set of keys and pressing them into Julie's hands. 'I don't like to ask you, but see that girl over there?' He pointed to a young woman who was leaning against a wall, looking dazed. 'She is my niece. It's her I came to find here. She is alone. Please, could you take her home? See that she's all right? Tell her that I'll be back as soon as I can.'

He watched as his patient was loaded into the ambulance. Julie could see he was worried. For his patient, his niece, or both, Julie couldn't be sure.

'Okay,' she said, a little reluctantly. She would much rather have followed up the patient in hospital. Perhaps assisted in Theatre—if the DJ made it that far. Still, she could hardly refuse her new boss's request—and he was probably right about space in the ambulance. Besides, she did need to make Richard sure and his friends were reunited with their parents, who…she glanced at her watch…should be arriving to collect them any time now.

'Thank you,' Pierre said softly, just before the doors of the ambulance closed. 'I owe you a favour,'

As soon as the ambulance pulled away, with its lights flashing and siren blaring, Julie crossed over to Pierre's niece. The girl looked up at Julie's approach.

'He's gone to the hospital, then?' The girl nodded in the direction of the departing ambulance. The words were slightly slurred. Had she been drinking? Julie wondered. Apart from that, and an ashen pallor to her skin, she looked okay.

'Yes, he had to. He asked if I could take you home. He's concerned about you. Are you okay? Has someone checked you over?'

The girl took a deep, shuddering breath. 'I'm fine. A bit shook up, but that's all. I was outside when the alarms went off. Is the person in the ambulance going to be all right?'

'I hope so,' Julie said. 'He's getting the best possible care.

I'm Julie, by the way.' She held out her hand to the girl who shook it reluctantly.

'Caroline,' the girl replied shortly.

'If you wouldn't mind waiting just a few minutes while I check on the guys I came with? Then I'll drive you home.' Julie said.

'Whatever,' the girl said. 'But really you don't have to take me home. I'm quite able to look after myself. Uncle Pierre treats me like a kid.' Caroline's mouth was set in a sullen line

'Please,' Julie said, 'let's just do as he asks. He's my boss and if I don't see you home I'll be in trouble.'

Caroline gave a loud theatrical sigh. 'He's *such* a bully. But okay—I'll wait here for you.'

It only took a couple of minutes for Julie to check on her young charges. Although still shocked, their fright was beginning to wear off and turn to excitement. Their parents had begun to arrive and, seeing that Richard's parents had everything under control, Julie returned to Caroline. She was relieved to find that she had waited for her. Somehow she wouldn't have put it past the girl to have sneaked off while her back was turned.

'Do you know where your uncle's car is parked?' Julie asked. Caroline pointed in the direction of a low-slung sports car across the road. Julie whistled under her breath. She had always wanted to drive once of those. She grinned at Caroline.

'He does have some pluses,' she said, and Julie briefly caught a glimmer of a smile.

'C'mon, then,' she said. 'Let's get you home.'

CHAPTER TWO

'WHERE to?' Julie asked Caroline as she eased the car into the traffic. Although it was late, the city centre was busy with late-night partygoers, many of whom had come to investigate what was going on. Caroline named a street that made Julie gasp. It was commonly known as Millionaires' Row by the locals.

'Is that where your parents live?' Julie glanced at Caroline and there was just enough light from the streetlamps for Julie to catch the wave of grief that crossed the girl's features.

'My parents are dead,' Caroline said flatly. 'They died in an accident.'

Julie slid a hand across and briefly grasped the girl's cold fingers in hers.

'I am so sorry,' she said. 'I know what that feels like. I lost my mother a couple of years ago and my father a few months after.' She still missed them both terribly. 'When did it happen?' she asked gently.

'Just after Christmas,' Caroline said softly.

Only a few weeks ago, then. Julie knew how raw her grief would still be.

'Do you have brothers or sisters?'

'I'm an only child,' Caroline responded.

Just like me, then, Julie thought, already feeling herself drawn to the young woman. It seemed they had a lot in common.

'It's why Uncle Pierre has come to stay,' Caroline continued after a pause. 'He lives in France. He's French, like my father is…was.' Her breath was ragged as she corrected herself. 'I told Pierre I was old enough to live by myself, but he wouldn't have it. Said it was impossible.' She pouted. 'He hardly knows me and now he is here bossing me about—interfering in my life.'

'But no one should be alone after such a terrible loss. I'm sure he just wants to help.'

'He never bothered with us before. Dad was always asking him to come and visit, but he was always too busy. Eventually my parents went to visit him. And now they're dead. If they hadn't gone—if he had come to see them instead like he should have—they'd still be all right. He is so unbelievably selfish.'

Julie was taken aback by the anger in Caroline's voice. But then she remembered how after *her* accident, when she'd felt she had been robbed of everything she'd thought mattered, she too had been angry, pushing away everyone, even her parents. And when a few years later her parents had died, she had thought she could never feel happy again. She too had been angry with the world at first. It had seemed so unfair.

'How old are you?'

'Seventeen. I'll be eighteen in a couple of months.'

Julie was surprised. Made up as Caroline was, she could have easily passed for twenty—older even.

'And you were out at the club by yourself?'

'Pierre didn't want me to go on my own. But he just doesn't understand…' She tailed off and looked out the window.

'Go on,' Julie prompted gently.

'My friends would have come with me. They're always asking me to go out with them. But even though they mean well, I get tired of their sympathy. They're always asking how I am. Am I okay? How am I doing? But they just don't get it—that all I want to do is forget. Just for a little while. Is that so awful?'

'No,' Julie said softly. 'It's not awful at all. Sometimes we all need to forget about stuff that hurts us.'

'I slipped away when his back was turned.' Caroline admitted. 'I left him a note telling him where I was and not to worry about me. But he came after me anyway. So embarrassing to be treated like a kid.'

Julie hid a smile. She was having no difficulty imaging the friction between the two. In many ways Caroline reminded her of herself as a teenager.

'But he was sort of right, wasn't he? Look what occurred back there. You could have been hurt. I'm sure he would never have forgiven himself if anything happened to you.' Julie shivered, remembering. 'I was terrified. Weren't you?'

'When the worst thing possible has already happened to you, there's not much that frightens you,' Caroline said softly, rubbing her eyes with the heels of her hands, and Julie's heart went out to her. 'I'm sorry,' she continued, regaining her composure. 'I don't usually go on like this. I think I must be more shaken than I thought. Anyway, I'm completely fine now, and that's what matters. I would have taken a taxi home perfectly easily, so he's fussing over nothing.'

Julie knew there was little point in pursuing the conversation. It was between Caroline and her uncle. The two women sat in silence for a few moments.

Caroline looked at Julie curiously.

'What happened to your face?' she said.

As usual, whenever someone reminded her of her scar, Julie's hand went to her cheek. Sometimes, not often, she managed to forget.

'Skiing accident,' she said, 'when I was about your age.'

'You should ask Uncle Pierre to fix you,' Caroline said, and this time Julie heard the note of pride that had crept into her voice.

Fix me? Julie thought. She didn't think anyone could *fix* her.

'He's a famous surgeon in France, you know,' Caroline added.

'So I gather,' Julie said dryly. 'However, I'm used to my face the way it is.'

But as she said the words she knew she was lying. She hated the scar.

They pulled up outside the address Caroline had given her. The house was an impressive detached sandstone building with a driveway large enough to hold several cars. Caroline showed her how to operate the gate from a button on the keyring, the gates swung open and Julie drew up beside the front door.

Caroline eased herself out of the car.

'Thank you for bringing me home,' she said politely.

'Will you be all right on your own?' Julie asked, unsure what to do. Should she go in with the girl? Wait for Pierre to return home? 'Would you like me to come in? I could wait with you until your uncle gets back.'

Caroline shook her head with a disdainful lift of her brow.

'There is no need. Please, you did what you said you'd do. I'll be perfectly fine.' Then her features softened. 'I'm sorry,' she said. 'I don't mean to be rude when you've been so kind. And I didn't mean to offload on you like that. I think it was the fright.'

'Hey, it's okay,' Julie said. 'I understand. Are you sure you don't want me to come in?'

Caroline shook her head again. 'I'm going to go straight to bed.' Julie knew she could hardly force her way into the house. So after a brief goodnight, and watching until Caroline was safely inside, she turned the car in the direction of the hospital. She was wide awake and knew sleep would be impossible, so she did what she always did when sleep eluded her—she went in search of work.

A and E was bustling with activity. A number of the clubgoers were being treated with minor injuries or for the effects of smoke inhalation. Julie found her friend Kim, one of the A and E nurses, gulping a cup of coffee at the nurses' station.

'Is there anything I can do to help?' Julie asked.

'Good grief, woman, do you tune into the police radio or what? How come you always seem to know when we have a rush on? Don't you have a life?' Kim stifled a yawn. She was always scolding Julie for working too hard, telling her she should get out more. Julie just ignored her friend's good-natured cajoling. It was her life, not Kim's, and she would live it the way she wanted to.

'I was at the club,' Julie said. 'Yes, really. And dancing!' She ignored her friend's look of feigned astonishment. 'I'm looking for one of the victims. The DJ. He was pretty badly burnt. Dr Favatier brought him in.'

'Ah, the divine Dr Favatier,' Kim sighed, rinsing her mug at the sink. 'I'd heard about him from some of the other nurses—and they weren't exaggerating. He is hot!' She gave herself a little shake, then grinned at Julie. 'But what am I thinking? And me a happily married woman and all.'

Her expression turned serious. 'Your DJ—his name's Tom Blackheath—is still in Resus. It's been chaos in here the last few hours—since even before the fire. This is the first chance I've had to draw breath.' She set her mug on the counter. 'Let's go find out how your injured DJ is.'

Tom was the only patient in the resuscitation room. There were several doctors and nurse working over him, Pierre included.

Tom had been sedated and ventilated and was still holding his own. Julie stood back from the gurney, not wanting to get in the way. She watched as Pierre checked the incisions and conferred with the A and E consultant. Eventually he noticed Julie. He seemed surprised to see her.

'You managed to get Caroline safely home, then?' he asked, turning peeling off his latex gloves and tossing them in the bin. When Julie nodded he continued.

'Thank you, but you didn't need to bring the car back here. I would have collected it tomorrow.'

Although it was after two in the morning and he was developing stubble, which only added to his dark good looks, he didn't seem tired. Quite the opposite, in fact. He radiated energy and vitality that pulsated through the room. Immediately something clicked inside Julie. Despite his image, here was someone who felt the same way about the job as she did. It was where they belonged—where they felt most alive.

His dark hair had flopped across his forehead and for one heady moment Julie was tempted to reach across and push it away from his eyes. Horrified at the thoughts that were flitting through her mind, she forced the image out of her head. What was she doing? Fantasising about her boss? It was totally inappropriate! Besides, she hardly needed to remind herself a man like this wouldn't be interested in someone like her.

'Yup, she wouldn't let me come in. I hope it was all right to leave her?' Julie prayed she wasn't blushing. He was probably used to women getting flustered in his presence but she was damned if she was going let him see how much he affected her.

'She is a very stubborn girl,' Pierre replied grimly. 'Takes after her father.'

He turned to the A and E consultant. 'I'll operate tomorrow,' he said, 'if he pulls through. In the meantime, I'm off to bed. Unless you would like any more help?' Satisfied he was no longer needed, he steered Julie away from the resus room.

'Are you ready to go?' he said. 'I'll run you home.'

'I'd rather stay and help,' she said.

He looked at her sharply, narrowing his eyes. 'If you remember, you are joining my team tomorrow…' He glanced at his watch. 'This morning. *De bleu!* It is almost three. You need your rest.'

'I don't need much sleep,' Julie protested.

'You do if you are working with me,' he said firmly.

Julie ignored him and nodded backwards in the direction of Tom. 'How is he?' she asked.

Just for a moment Pierre looked tired. He rubbed a hand across his cheek. 'The next twenty-four hours are critical. If they manage to stabilise him—if he survives—we'll start doing skin grafts later on today. You can assist, if you like.'

'I'd appreciate that,' she said quietly. 'I would like to see his treatment through. I feel I owe it to him,'

Pierre looked at her intently. 'I'll need you alert and under control,' he said. 'There's no room for emotion in the theatre,' he said.

Julie realised it was pointless to argue. He had completely misunderstood what she had meant. Suddenly the adrenaline seeped away, and she felt exhausted.

'You don't have to take me home,' she said. 'I'll get a taxi.'

The last thing she wanted right at this moment was to find herself in close proximity to this man. A good night's sleep, or at least a few hours—and there was hardly enough time to get more than that now—would be enough for her to pull herself together and get her emotions under control.

'Of course I am going to take you home. It is the least I can do.' He held out his hand. For a stunned moment Julie thought he meant her to take his hand, and almost laid hers in his. Just in time she realised he was expecting his car keys but she was unable to prevent the tell-tale blush flooding her cheeks. Pierre looked at her quizzically, then grinned.

'You will be perfectly safe with me, Dr McKenzie, whatever people might say.'

Julie shot him a furious look before she could prevent herself and felt herself redden from the tips of her ears to the tips of her toes. Was he actually flirting with her? And what was worse, did he actually think she'd be flattered, grateful even?

'And why should I think I wouldn't be safe with you, Dr Favatier?' she asked in the coldest voice she could summon. He looked at her, then as recognition dawned his blue eyes glinted mischievously.

'Because people think I drive too fast, of course. What other reason could there be?'

Julie felt her skin shrink with embarrassment. *Great start, Dr McKenzie*, she thought. *Way to go, girl!*

* * *

Julie sank into the soft leather seat of Pierre's car. Asking her for her post code, he programmed it into the satellite navigation system of his car.

'It easier than you telling me how to get there,' he said, pulling out into the road. 'You did very well back there, at the fire.'

'I'm just glad you were there,' she said. 'I would have hated having to do a tracheostomy on my own.' She slid him a look. 'It's quite different having to do something out of the hospital setting.'

Pierre turned and flashed her a smile. 'Something tells me you would have coped okay,' he said. 'You stayed very cool.'

Julie felt herself glow at the praise. 'Skiing teaches you that. How to stay focussed, even when you're terrified. And I was,' she admitted.

'Then you hid it well,' he said. 'I think I'm going to like having you on my team.' He drove quickly through the now deserted streets. Julie was acutely conscious of his presence in the cramped interior of his car. Suddenly she felt awkward.

Glancing down at this hand on the gearstick, she noticed that his right hand had been burnt.

'You hurt your hand,' she said.

'It's nothing,' he said. 'I put some cream on. It will be fine.'

He smiled at her again, his eyes creasing at the corners. Julie felt a tingle run up her spine.

'Are all Scottish women so reckless?' he asked. 'You must know you risked your own life staying inside the burning building to help.'

Julie straightened in her seat. 'I only did what anyone would have done. I couldn't stand back and do nothing. I wasn't being *reckless*.'

'I know men who wouldn't have done what you did,' he argued.

'How people behave in a time of crisis has nothing to do with what sex they are!' Julie said crossly.

This time Pierre laughed out loud.

'Dis donc,' he said. 'So you say.'

Julie felt her skin prickle. He was mocking her. Despite finding him unnervingly attractive, she wondered if she actually liked her new boss—even if he was the kind of surgeon she aspired to be. He seemed to have a pretty sexist view of women. Perhaps that was down to the type of women he spent time with. Julie could just see him with a glamorous simpering model on his arm. Someone who hung onto his every word and liked to have doors opened and him order for her. Someone who was unlike her in every possible way.

'Anyway, you were pretty reckless yourself,' she said. 'You took a risk going to help the DJ.'

Pierre raised an eyebrow, his eyes silver in the semi-darkness. 'A chance you were about to take yourself. In fact, you would have taken a greater risk than I. You would have never been able to get him out of there. And somehow I suspect you would not have left him.'

Hearing the admiration in his voice, Julie felt somewhat mollified. But whatever he thought, she'd only done what anyone in her shoes would have done.

Happily, before she had a chance to think of a response they had pulled up outside her flat in the West End of Edinburgh.

She leapt out of the car, noticing Pierre's surprise at her almost indecent haste to get away.

'Thank you for the lift,' she said. 'I'll see you later this morning.' Without waiting for a reply, she turned and was relieved when she heard his car roar off into the night.

Pierre felt strangely unsettled as he drove home. Stopping at a traffic light, his eyes caught an enormous billboard straddling the pavement. The woman advertising a famous make of bath soap reminded him of someone. Almost at once he realised who—Julie. The model had the same glossy-brown hair, sweet smile and charcoal smudged grey eyes radiating warmth, compassion and intelligence.

He rubbed the tiredness from his eyes. Dr Julie McKenzie was brave and cool under pressure, qualities he knew were important in a surgeon, but it was the Julie the woman who intrigued him most. She seemed oblivious to how beautiful she was, even with the scar. Instead, she came across as shy and uncertain of herself as a woman. He couldn't help recalling the way she had blushed in his company. Had she'd been anyone else he would have felt flattered, even been tempted to show her how attractive she was. But she wasn't just anyone, he reminded himself. She was his colleague, his junior colleague, and therefore out of bounds. An affair with her was completely out of the question. And not just because she was a colleague but because he guessed she was not someone who would take any relationship lightly. For him, the only relationships he liked were the casual ones. All his lovers knew that. At least he assumed they all did. Until Monique, that was. She had chosen not to believe him even though he had made his position clear right at the start of their relationship. But when he had told her it was over, after it had run its course, she had been devastated and

furious. After the most embarrassing scene he had sworn he
would never get involved with a colleague again.

It was a pity about Julie, he thought. He had enough of
experience of women to suspect that underneath that shy
exterior lay a woman of passion. Not that she was really his
type. Not even remotely. Why, then, did the knowledge that
Julie was off limits leave him feeling bleaker than ever?

Julie yawned as she poured herself another cup of coffee in
the duty room. She finished looking over her patients' charts
as the other staff gathered together.

'He's gorgeous,' one of the staff nurses was saying to her
colleagues. 'And as for that accent...' She shivered with
delight. 'He could have his wicked way with me any time.'

Despite herself, Julie felt her ears prick up. It was obvious
who they were talking about.

'You'll need to get in line, then,' Dr Cramond, one of the
other junior doctors, replied.

She, unlike Julie, was pretty in that doll-like way most men
seemed to admire. She was probably just Pierre's type, Julie
thought, trying to ignore how envious the thought made her.

'Do you think he's attached, Julie?' Dr Cramond asked.

'Not a clue,' said Julie, returning to her notes. She really
didn't want to be drawn into a discussion about Pierre with her
new colleagues. Even if it made her seem a little standoffish.

'Bound to be,' said the nurse, a friendly looking woman
with glossy black hair who had introduced herself as Fiona.
'Very likely he has someone back in France.'

'But I gather he's not married,' Dr Cramond said wistfully,
'so as far as I am concerned that makes him fair game.'

They stopped talking abruptly when the man himself walked

into the duty room. Dressed in a dark grey suit that must have cost an arm and a leg, clean shaven and with just a hint of aftershave, Julie was struck again by his model good looks. He wouldn't look out of place on the cover of a magazine.

Julie replaced her cup and scrambled hastily to her feet.

'Good morning, Dr Favatier,' she said.

'Bonjour,' he replied. He glanced down at the sheaf of notes he held in his hand. 'Shall we get started?'

'Have you heard how our patient from last night is doing?' she asked as she and Fiona accompanied him across the ward.

'I saw him in Intensive Care this morning,' Pierre answered. 'He's stable. I plan to take him to Theatre later this morning. We'll go and see him again after rounds. But first let's see our elective patients.'

Pierre walked over to the first patient, a lady in her early sixties with short grey hair and a ready, if lopsided smile. *'Bonjour*, Madame Tulloch,' Pierre greeted her with a broad grin. 'I gather you know Staff Nurse already?' he said, indicating Fiona. 'And this is Dr McKenzie, who will be helping me look after you.'

'Good morning, Dr Favatier. It's nice to see you again, and to meet you, Dr McKenzie,' Mrs Tulloch responded. Despite her smile, Julie could say traces of anxiety in her faded blue eyes.

'Could you remind us of this lady's history, Dr McKenzie?' Pierre asked.

Julie had made sure that she had read up on all the patients earlier, having arrived at seven to give herself enough time.

'Mrs Tulloch saw her dentist for a routine check-up six months ago and he discovered a suspect growth on her jaw bone. He referred her to the surgeons, who identified a tumour. The surgeons removed the tumour and a piece of bone was taken from the left hip and grafted onto the jawbone. Mrs Tulloch has had two rounds of radiotherapy and is doing well, apart from some difficulty with speaking and swallowing.'

Pierre nodded approvingly. 'Well done, Dr McKenzie. Brief and to the point.' he said.

'Mrs Tulloch is scheduled for Theatre this morning,' Julie finished.

'How are you feeling, Mrs Tulloch?' Pierre asked the woman, who had been listening intently to Julie's résumé of her condition.

'I feel fine,' she said. 'A little anxious perhaps, but otherwise fine.' Although her words were slurred, Julie could understand her perfectly.

'You know we are planning to operate today?' Pierre told the woman. 'And while you might not get a full return of movement to your mouth, I am hoping for a great improvement.' He traced a gentle finger down her line of her jaw. 'We should also be able to improve the way the scar is pulling down the right side of your mouth.'

'It's not so much the way it makes me look,' Mrs Tulloch said. 'I know I should be grateful the operation was a success and I am grateful. It's just that it makes my speech and eating so awkward.'

Pierre turned to Julie, 'What do you think, Dr McKenzie?'

Julie bent over Mrs Tulloch. She asked her a few questions then, with the patient's permission, gently examined her jaw. The incision had healed well, but the scar tissue puckered the skin, pulling the mouth out of shape.

'Looks like Mrs Tulloch has made a good recovery from her initial surgery,' she said. Pierre passed her the X-ray, which clearly illuminated the tumour prior to surgery. He then passed her another film, which showed the jaw bone with the tumour removed and the grafted piece of bone.

'You were lucky that this was caught when it was.' Julie smiled down at the woman. 'And it looks as if the replaced bone in your jaw has healed well.'

'I do feel lucky. If I hadn't gone to the dentist that week…I nearly didn't, you know—too much going on—and if he hadn't been suspicious, it could have been a different story.'

'But it wasn't. It was caught it in time, and we'll soon have you looking as close to how you looked before. I can see you were a very attractive woman.' Pierre grinned at his patient.

Goodness! Julie thought. Did he flirt with everyone?

Mrs Tulloch smiled back crookedly. 'A long time ago perhaps, Dr Favatier. But it would be nice to look more normal again.'

With a few more words of reassurance Pierre moved away from the bedside and explained to Julie what they were planning to do in Theatre. 'Of course, you will just be assisting me, but I need you to do exactly as I tell you. I will be operating very close to one of the major facial nerves. We can't afford any damage there.'

They crossed the ward to speak to the second patient on their list. Julie looked at his chart. Mike Simpson was a twenty-three-year-old who had come off his motorbike the day before. He had lost a chunk of his calf in the collision and Pierre planned to graft some skin from his thigh to help the wound heal. Mike was sitting up in bed plugged in to his MP3 player, which he removed as soon as they approached.

Pierre talked the patient through what he planned to do later in Theatre.

'How long before I can go biking again?' Mike asked. 'It's pretty boring being cooped up inside while all my mates are out having fun.'

'I'd give it at least four weeks for the graft to heal,' Pierre replied. 'But your broken leg will take longer.'

'You haven't been put off, then?' Julie asked. She knew from the notes that Mike had been lucky to escape with his life from the accident.

'You've got to be kidding!' Mike replied. 'The insurance has already said they'll pay out and I've decided which new bike to buy. A Kawasaki 750. I've always wanted one of those beauties.'

'I've got a Harley Davidson. I brought it with me from France.' Pierre said, and as the men launched into a discussion on the various advantages of different motorbikes, Fiona and Julie exchanged a look. Julie knew how Mike felt. After her accident she couldn't wait to get back on her skis. Being near death's door wasn't what had stopped her from skiing competitively—it had simply been that her accident had meant that she'd had too much time off training to be selected for the Olympic squad. That had been almost the worst thing about the accident. All those years of training, getting up in the small hours of the morning to go to the slopes, leaving her parents from a very young age to go abroad to train—all of it—for nothing. Still, she couldn't regret everything about it. If she hadn't had the accident she would never gone in for medicine. And now she couldn't imagine any other life.

Their next patient was in the paediatric ward. Shona was a girl of ten who was scheduled for an operation to have her ears pinned back. She was shy and clearly overawed by her surroundings. Her anxious mother sat by her bedside, reading to her from a book.

'Phillip Pullman,' Julie said reading the title. 'He used to be one of my favourite writers. Still is.' She grinned down at the young girl, who smiled back.

'But you're a grown-up,' she said.

'I think his books are so good anyone can read them, don't you?'

While Julie distracted the young girl, Pierre finished examining Shona's ears.

'You know what we are going to do, *petite*?' he said.

She nodded.

'And you are certain that this is what you want?'

The girl glanced at her mother, before nodding. Pierre frowned and looked enquiringly at the mother.

'You know, Shona,' Julie said gently, 'you don't have to have the operation if you don't want to. It's not a big operation— not at all—but, still, if you'd rather not…'

The mother glanced at Julie. 'I've told her so many times,' she said, 'that there is nothing wrong with her ears.' She leaned across and stroked her daughter's head.

'You are such a pretty girl, no one will even notice your ears,' Pierre said. 'We discussed this when I saw you yesterday. You know you can still change your mind?'

The girl looked at the three adults and folded her arms across her chest, a mutinous line to her mouth.

'I want this operation. They tease me at school. They call me Dumbo!' Her voice dropped to a whisper. 'You don't know what it's like to be teased because of the way you look.' As she said the words she looked at Julie and her hand flew to her mouth in horror. 'I'm sorry…I mean…' she stumbled.

It took every ounce of Julie's willpower not to raise her hand and cover her scar. Instead she sat down on the edge of the bed.

'No one teases me,' she said. 'At least, not to my face. They wouldn't dare. But I do know what it's like to feel self-conscious about the way you look. It can hurt when people stare at you.'

Shona nodded, clearly gratified that someone understood. Pierre was watching Julie closely.

'So if you are sure that this is what you want, that is fine. As I said, it's not a big operation, but you'll be sore for a while.' Julie repeated.

'I want it,' Shona said.

'Then you shall have it, of course,' Pierre said. 'I just wanted you to know that you could still change your mind.'

Pierre and Julie left Fiona finalising the patients' prep for theatre.

'Let's go and see Tom in ITU,' Pierre suggested. 'I've added him to the end of the list. His operation is the trickiest and most time-consuming.'

As they made their way towards Intensive Care, Pierre stopped and turned to Julie. He lifted long fingers to her face and gently felt along the ridge of her scar. It was all Julie could do not to flinch, but whether it was from embarrassment or the electric tingle she felt from his fingertips, she didn't want to hazard a guess.

'What happened?' he asked softly, dropping his hand to his side.

'Accident at speed. While I was skiing,' she said

His mouth relaxed.

'Now, why am I not surprised? It seems to me you are someone who enjoys danger,' he said. 'Going too fast, I think?'

'It was part of it. I had to go fast. I was training for the woman's downhill. For the Winter Olympics.'

Pierre's eyebrows shot up. He let out a low whistle. 'Why did you stop competing? Was it because of the accident?'

'Yes, I had missed too much training so I was dropped from the team. I still ski, although now it's only for pleasure. I go up north—usually to the Cairngorms—whenever I get the chance.'

Together they started walking again. Julie was relieved that they had moved on from discussing her face, although she found talking about her aborted skiing hopes no less distressing.

'I'd heard one could ski in Scotland, but I didn't really believe it. I didn't think there was enough snow.' Pierre said, sounding surprised. 'I would like to see for myself if it is still possible.'

'Oh, there's plenty of snow still if that's what you're worried about.' Julie reassured him. 'We haven't had much the last few seasons, but this year's made up for it in spades.'

Pierre frowned. 'In spades? What do spades have to do with skiing?'

Julie laughed. 'I'm sorry. It's an idiom. It just means there is plenty of something—in this case snow.' Amazingly she found herself beginning to relax in his company.

Pierre stopped outside the door of ITU. He looked down at her, his blue eyes searching her face. 'I should like to see you ski,' he said. Something in his tone made Julie's heart thump. 'Perhaps you could show me these Scottish mountains of yours one day?'

Confused at the turn the conversation was taking, Julie could only nod. Was he asking her out?

'I have skied all my life,' he went on. 'But I haven't had much chance recently. I find it's a good way to relax and I know Caroline would like to learn,' he said, looking thoughtful. 'Maybe it could be something she and I could do together.'

Of course, Julie thought. *He was thinking about his niece. Not her.* Acutely aware of feeling irrationally disappointed, she was relieved when he turned away towards Tom's bed.

The DJ was still sedated, and was being monitored by an intensive care nurse called Linda, whom Julie had met several times before when she'd been on General Surgical.

'He's pretty strong,' Linda told Pierre and Julie, sounding pleased. 'We think he's got a good chance of pulling through.'

Julie caught her breath when she looked down at the injured man. Swathed in bandages and with tubes everywhere, he looked in no fit state to be operated on.

'Shouldn't the grafts wait until he's recovered?' she asked Pierre.

'The sooner we start doing the grafts the better, believe me,' he replied. 'When so much of the skin has been destroyed, there is nothing left to heal and cover the open tissue. As it is, it will take a number of operations before we replace enough skin.'

As they were making plans for Tom's future surgery, a young woman with frantic red eyes underscored with dark circles approached the bedside. She had obviously flung on the first thing that had come to hand—crumpled jogging pants and a T-shirt. *She looks out of her mind with worry*, Julie thought.

'This is Tom's girlfriend, Trudi. Trudi, this is Drs Favatier and McKenzie,' Linda introduced them.

'How is he?' Trudi whispered. 'Please, tell me he's going to be all right.' She blinked , struggling to hold back the tears.

'Trudi has been here for most of the night,' Linda explained. 'I've tried to persuade her to go and get some rest, but she won't hear of it.'

'I don't want to leave him,' Trudi said. 'I only went to get some coffee to help me stay awake. I'm petrified something will happen to him while I'm not here.'

'We're not going to let anything happen to him,' Pierre said firmly. 'Not after he's made it this far.'

'You're the doctor who saved his life!' Trudi said. 'They told me it was the French doctor that pulled him out.' She looked up at Pierre, her eyes shining with unshed tears. 'Thank you. Thank you so much. I'll never forget what you did.'

Pierre shuffled his feet. 'Dr McKenzie was there too,' he said. 'She spotted him in trouble, and she would have risked her own life to save him. It's her you should be thanking, not me.'

Linda's gaze swung from Pierre to Julie. Julie sensed that this was the first time she had heard about their involvement in the fire and guessed it would be all over the hospital by lunchtime. Inwardly she cringed. She hated drawing attention to herself.

Trudi turned to Julie and grasped her hands. 'I'll never forget either of you,' she said fiercely. 'Never.'

'Please,' Julie said, embarrassed. 'I didn't do very much.' She looked at Pierre in desperation, and was grateful when he seemed to pick up on her extreme discomfort.

'We will talk again later. After the operation,' he said gently. 'In the meantime, Dr McKenzie and I are due in Theatre.'

'So that's four patients we have in Theatre altogether,' he

said as they headed out of ITU. 'Although Shona's operation will be quick, the other two will take up the rest of the session. Then lastly we have Tom.' He glanced at his watch. 'Theatre starts in an hour, so I suggest if you haven't had something to eat, you get something now. We could be in Theatre for the rest of the day.' He hesitated. 'You know, if you wish, I could operate on that scar for you. I do a lot of cosmetic surgery back in France.'

Julie raised her hand to cover the scar. 'I am happy with my face the way it is,' she said stiffly.

Pierre reached out and, taking her hand, gently pulled it away. 'It *is* a beautiful face,' he said, looking her directly in her eyes. He was so close she could almost distinguish the individual eyelashes framing his deep blue eyes. Eyelashes like that were wasted on a man, she thought, trying to ignore the way her heart had started galloping. Then what he had said sank in. He had called her beautiful. Her heart beat even faster. Did he really believe that? She gave herself a mental shake. No, of course he didn't, he was just being kind. It was far more likely that he just couldn't stop himself from complimenting every woman who crossed his path.

'Your bone structure is perfect,' he continued, scrutinising her face with a professional eye. 'You are lucky. No amount of plastic surgery can ever improve on that.'

So it wasn't really her he was seeing after all! To him she was just another surgical problem he could solve. 'I'll see you in Theatre,' she said abruptly, wanting nothing more than to get away from him so she could still her pounding heart. Without waiting for his reply, she turned on her heel and left him standing in the corridor looking bemused.

* * *

In Theatre Pierre appeared even more assured and confident than ever. Despite herself Julie was very conscious of the dark hairs on his bronze chest that she could see from the V in his scrub top. Only his eyes were visible as they glittered above his mask, and Julie was beginning to develop the uncomfortable feeling, as they drilled into hers, that he could read her thoughts. The thought made her cringe. The last thing she wanted her boss to know was that she, like every other woman, was not immune to his stunning looks and the charisma enveloped him like a cloak. Kim was right. She needed to get a life, she thought with exasperation, before forcing her attention back to the operation. And she needed to concentrate. Regardless of how Pierre viewed her as a woman, above all else she wanted him to think highly of her as a clinician.

The operations went well and Julie was surprised when she looked up at the clock on the theatre wall to find it was long past five o'clock. She had to admit that, despite his film-star good looks, Pierre was a highly skilled surgeon. Every stroke of the scalpel was sure and confident and, unlike some of the surgeons Julie had worked with, he never seemed impatient when staff were slow to respond to his instructions.

Before they'd started, Pierre had asked for a CD of Rachmaninov's third piano concerto to be played. Of course he wasn't to know the twentieth-century Russian composer was one of Julie's favourites. As he'd operated, he'd patiently explained to Julie every step of what he was doing. Even when she had fumbled a little with the retractors, he had smiled and simply corrected the movement of her hands. As Theatre progressed, Julie found herself anticipating what he wanted her to do before he asked her. It Theatre at least it seemed as if they were in synch.

When it was Shona's turn to be wheeled into Theatre, Pierre replaced the Rachmaninov CD with a favourite of the little girl's. Shona recognised the music straight away and immediately relaxed, chatting with the theatre staff about her favourite bands. Even when the young girl succumbed to the anaesthetic, Pierre insisted that they leave Shona's music playing. His thoughtfulness impressed her. Maybe there was more to Pierre Favatier than met the eye.

Eventually, later that day, when Tom had been wheeled out of Theatre and into Recovery, Pierre stripped off his gloves and gown and tossed them into the bin.

'Well done, everyone,' he said, before addressing Julie directly. 'Dr McKenzie, it seems you have the makings of a plastic surgeon.'

Julie was pleased at his praise, although she hadn't done much except assist. 'You can do the next otoplasty if you like,' Pierre had continued.

'Thank you,' Julie said simply. But she was secretly delighted to know he had confidence in her ability.

'You should go home to rest,' he added. 'There's another list tomorrow. I'll see you at rounds?'

'I'll check on the patients first, make sure they have enough pain relief,' Julie said.

'There is no need. I am happy to check on them. It's been a long day and after last night you must be tired.'

'I'd rather,' Julie said. 'I like to see my patients settled on the ward before I leave for the day.'

Pierre flashed his perfect white teeth at her. 'Stubborn, just as I suspected,' he said. 'But don't you have someone, a boyfriend perhaps, waiting for you at home?' Julie was annoyed to find herself blushing again. Really, it was about time she grew out of this juvenile habit.

'No, not at the moment,' she said, resisting the impulse to remind him that whether she had a boyfriend or not was none of his business. 'All I have is a date with the library and a large number of reference books on plastic surgery.' Now, why had she said that? It made her sound such a loser.

Pierre looked at her, seeming unusually indecisive.

'How would you feel about joining Caroline and I for dinner tomorrow evening?' He held up a hand as Julie started to protest. 'Please? You would be doing me a big favour,' he said. He ran a rueful hand through his shock of dark hair and Julie was amused to see a lock stand up like a question mark but dismayed to find that she found him even more attractive looking less than immaculate. Was he asking her for a date? Had his question about boyfriends been more than a casual enquiry? Julie's heart skipped a beat.

'Caroline and I struggle to find things to talk about,' he continued. 'She seems to have taken to you, though. In fact, it was her who suggested I invite you. She is worried that she was a little offhand with you last night after your kindness to her.'

Julie's heart sank. So it had been Caroline's idea? How could she have been so stupid to have thought—even for a moment—that it was Pierre who wanted her company?

'It would make dinner—how do you say?—less...' He seemed to struggle to find the right word. 'Uncomfortable if you were there.' He looked at Julie almost pleadingly. Something in the blue eyes and the self-deprecating grin was melting Julie's resolve. But she really didn't feel up to spending more time in this man's company. Not when he made her feel so…what was the word she was looking for? Hundreds sprang to mind. Out of her depth, breathless, dizzy, inexperienced, gauche, edgy—the list was endless, she thought wryly.

Noticing her hesitation, he went on. 'We can go over recent cases after dinner, if you like.' He was almost pleading Julie thought, wondering.

She felt herself weaken. She could just about resist Dr Favatier the playboy, but this Pierre, the one who seemed to need her help, that was more difficult.

Besides, there was something about Caroline that had struck a chord with her. In Caroline, she recognised the same aching loneliness that she had felt since her parents had died. She missed being part of a family and knew Caroline would be feeling the same. However much she wanted to keep her distance from Pierre, she knew she couldn't ignore the teenager's silent plea for help.

'Where and when?' she asked, capitulating.

He looked relieved. 'The house—you remember where it is?' At Julie's nod he continued, '*D'accord*. I'm cooking. If you come about half past seven, that should give us both enough time.'

CHAPTER THREE

KIM lounged on Julie's bed as Julie put the finishing touches to her make-up.

'Dinner at the gorgeous Dr Favatier's home?' her friend teased. 'Do you know how many women would kill to be in your shoes?'

Julie peered at her reflection in the mirror. If she applied any more foundation to her face, she'd look like someone made up for a pantomime. She took a tissue and started scrubbing it off.

'It's not a date,' Julie insisted. 'The only reason I've been invited is because of his niece. Don't think for one minute he wants me there for any other purpose.'

'C'mon, Julie, you're so obsessed with that scar you forget that you are a beautiful woman. The scar's hardly noticeable— I keep telling you but you won't believe me. What's more, anyone would kill for your cheekbones. And as for those lips—Julia Roberts, watch out!'

It was the second time in as many days that Julie had been called beautiful. She stared at her image in the mirror. Large, solemn grey eyes stared back. Her eyes were probably her best feature, Julie admitted—that and her chestnut-coloured hair. All the better for hiding behind, she thought grimly. And as for her mouth, she had always considered it too large. No. She wasn't and never had been beautiful. Not even before the accident. But it was kind of her friend to try and make her feel better.

'Mmm, so you say. But you have to admit I haven't exactly had men beating a path to my door,' Julie protested.

'What about Dave? And Robert? And Bob?'

'They weren't my type. And I don't call being asked out by three men in three years having men beat a path to the door,' Julie replied.

'Only because you wouldn't have it any other way. You are *so* fussy. And I'm sure you'd be asked out by hundreds more if you just encouraged them, instead of frightening them off with one I'm-not-available-to you look.'

Julie snorted in disbelief. 'I do not!'

But Kim hadn't finished. 'What is even worse for us shorties are those legs that go up to your armpits. So unfair.'

Julie had to laugh at her friend's aggrieved expression. 'Hey, you aren't bad looking yourself!' It was a blatant under-statement. Kim, olive skin, luxuriant dark hair and vivacious personality, attracted the opposite sex like bees to a honey pot. However, Julie knew she only had eyes for her husband and she envied their deep love for each other.

Nevertheless, Kim stood and surveyed herself critically in the mirror. 'At least, John likes a few curves. At least he says he does. Just as well. I don't think I could give up chocolate. Even for him.'

'No woman should have to give up chocolate for any man,' Julie agreed, smiling broadly.

'So what gives, then? Why precisely are you going to

have dinner with Pierre? Tell me again exactly what he said,'
Kim persisted.

'Just that Caroline would like me to come over and have
dinner with them. I gather the relationship with his niece isn't
the easiest, and I think he imagines having someone there to
act as a buffer will help. She's still grieving for her parents.
You should see her, Kim—she's like a lost soul. She reminds
me so much of myself when I was her age.'

'You could never resist a person in trouble, could you?'
Kim teased. 'You're always collecting them.' She counted off
on her fingers. 'Richard, Lexy, now Caroline. And that's just
for starters.'

'That is so not true!' Julie disagreed hotly. 'I like Richard—
he's good fun. And as for Lexy—I need her more than she
needs me. She's more like a mother than a friend. I guess
they've all become my family. Between them, you and my
work, I am happy.' Impulsively Julie hugged her. 'I don't
need a man in my life.'

'So you keep saying. I think it's more to do with not
wanting to risk being hurt again.' Kim's face grew serious.
'But you can't hide away from life for ever, Julie.'

Julie scowled at her friend, warning her to change the
subject. But it seemed Kim wasn't about to stop yet. 'How
old do you think the delectable Pierre is?'

'Thirty-something? He'd have to be at least that to be in
the position he is now,' Julie replied, resigned.

'They say he's well known throughout the medical world.
Not to mention extremely rich. Not married either, as far as
we can tell. So he's perfect for you, Jules.'

'It sounds as if the gossips are having a field day,' Julie said
disapprovingly. 'And how many times do I have to tell you I

am the last person he'd be interested in? More to the point—
he's not my type either.'

'Oh?' Kim stopped rummaging through Julie's wardrobe.
'Here, put this on. It shows off your legs.' She tossed a shift
dress towards Julie. Despite its plainness, it was beautifully
cut and Kim was right—it did show off her figure. She caught
the dress just before it hit the floor. 'And why *exactly* is he
not your type? What is there not to like? You can hardly call
him immature,' her friend persisted.

Julie slipped on the dress. It was one of her favourites. And
it was simple enough for it not to look as if she was dressing up.

'One. You say he's rich. Okay, so how did he make his
money? Probably by encouraging women to have surgery
they don't need. Two. He's unattached. I wonder why that
should be? As you pointed out, it's unlikely that it's down to
lack of choice. Three… I'm sure there must be a third. I just
can't think of it at the moment.' All the same, Julie wondered
if she was being truthful with herself. The main reason she
didn't want to think of Pierre in that way was because she
knew deep in her heart it was pointless. She had had her heart
broken once before by someone she'd thought had loved her
unconditionally. And if Luke hadn't been able to accept the
way she looked, no man, least of all Dr Pierre Favatier, would
ever be interested in her. And if the knowledge caused her
heart to tighten, well, she had accepted marriage and children
were not for her. Hadn't she?

On the way to her dinner engagement, Julie called in at St
Margaret's Hospice. Although some people might have found
it depressing, Julie found it quite the opposite. The building
itself was warm and cosy and the staff fantastic—all of them,

but in particular the head nurse, Audrey, whom Julie had come to know well and admired enormously.

The last few weeks of her mother's life had been spent at St Margaret's. Julie had wanted to keep her mother at home, to look after her herself, but her mother had insisted that it was too much for Julie and her father, particularly with the hours Julie had to put in at the hospital. It had been at the hospice that Julie had met Richard and got to know Lexy.

She found who she was looking for in one of the side rooms. Lexy Dunlop had been a code breaker at Bletchley Park during the war. Despite her advanced years and her illness, she had a lively sense of humour and a keen interest in the lives of everyone around her. In the months since Julie had come to know her, she had come love her. She made a determined effort to visit a least a couple of times a week.

'Ah, it's Dr McKenzie come to see me,' Lexy said, looking delighted to see Julie. Then she narrowed her eyes. 'And all dressed up and looking hot! So who's the lucky man, then?'

Julie grinned at her elderly friend's terminology. Beside her bed lay her latest acquisition—her mobile phone. She always insisted that getting old was no reason not to stay up to date— or 'with it', as she insisted on saying. Julie perched on the bed.

'What makes you think I'm dressed up for a man?' she asked

'Because, my dear, I have lived too long not to recognise a twinkle in a girl's eye when I see it! Besides, in all the time you've come to see me, you've never looked as animated as you do now. Come on, spill the beans. Who has made you light up like a Christmas tree?'

'I'm sorry to disappoint you, but it's not a date. I'm going to dinner with my boss and his niece. And it was her who invited me,' she said defensively. Why was everyone so determined to get her paired off?

Lexy narrowed her eyes suspiciously. 'But, correct me if I'm wrong, your boss is good looking and unattached?'

Julie blushed.

'Okay, I admit he's good looking—I'm not so sure about the unattached bit. But he's not my type and I am certainly not his.'

'Is he some kind of ogre? Is that why he's not your type?'

Julie laughed. 'I've just had this conversation with my friend Kim. No, he's not a monster. He's a terrific doctor who seems to really care about his patients.'

'Then what is the problem?

'Dr Favatier is the type of man who has a different woman on his arm every week. Your typical playboy. He'd never look twice at me,' Julie said forlornly. 'Not that I'd want him to,' she added hastily, wagging her finger at Lexy. 'So I don't want you getting any ideas.'

'And why do you think he wouldn't find you attractive? I keep telling you that scar you keep going on about is hardly noticeable. It doesn't stop anyone from seeing the stunning woman you are.'

'I wish people would stop saying that,' Julie said hotly. 'I know they're just trying to be kind. But it doesn't help. Why does everyone talk to me as if they know what is best for me?' She was thinking back to what Pierre had said about operating on her face. As if only perfection would do. 'Why can't everyone accept I'm happy with my life just the way it is?'

'People say it because it is true,' Lexy said quietly. 'Perhaps its time you believed them. And, no,' she continued, 'when I look into your eyes and see the sadness that is always lurking just below the surface, however much you try to disguise it, I cannot believe you are happy. However much I want to.'

'You are wrong, Lexy. I have everything I need in my life. I have you for a start, my work, my friends.' Julie leaned down and kissed the old lady's cheek. 'Oh, Lexy, what would I do without you? But can we please change the subject?'

Lexy patted her hand. 'And me without you,' she said quietly. 'I know you have your own very busy life without taking time out to visit an old, sick lady.'

'I'm the lucky one,' Julie insisted. Glancing at her watch, she was horrified to find it was after seven. She stood. 'But I'm going to have to go if I'm not to be late. I'll see you soon.'

At half past seven on the dot Julie arrived outside Caroline's house. A light dusting of snow had begun to fall and Julie felt a pang of longing for the mountains in the north. On the slopes was really the only time she felt free and totally un-selfconscious. The skiing would be fantastic now, she knew. It would be her weekend off, so perhaps she should leave on Friday night for the mountains? Book into the B&B she used whenever she was on her own? She'd have all day Saturday and maybe even Sunday morning to ski.

When Pierre opened the door to her Julie caught her breath. He looked annoyingly, jaw-droppingly handsome, dressed in a tight-fitting V neck sweater and faded blue jeans, which emphasised his lean, muscular frame. His thick black hair was still damp from his shower and as Julie squeezed past him she caught a whiff of expensive aftershave. Although she had taken time over her appearance, combing her hair over to one side in a futile attempt to hide her scar, she felt gauche and plain next to his easy assurance.

Pierre smiled at her and her heart missed a beat. *Get a grip, girl*, she told herself. *You are here for a purpose—not a date.*

He led her through to the sitting room. Someone with fantastic taste had furnished the room, Julie thought appreciatively, noting the fine rosewood antiques and comfortable sofas. An open fire blazed in the hearth and instinctively Julie went over to warm her hands. She let her eyes linger on a landscape by a Scottish artist that she had admired but never been able to afford.

'I love that artist—Iona McGruther, isn't it?' Julie crossed over to the painting and admired the artist's sure strokes and vibrant choice of colours.

'I'm glad you like it. Iona is…' His mouth twisted and a shadow crossed his features. 'Was Caroline's mother,' Pierre said quietly.

Julie's hand flew to her mouth. 'I'm sorry—I had no idea.' She shook her head sadly. 'She was a fantastic artist. What a loss to the art world.'

'Caroline told you, then?' he said.

'She only said that her parents had died recently and that you had come to Scotland to be with her.'

Pierre came to stand beside her. His eyes clouded over as he studied the painting with her.

'Iona worked mainly as an interior designer and she was only just gaining recognition in the art world,' he said softly, his voice underscored with traces of pain. 'Although she'd been painting for years—long before Caroline was born. Before she met my brother even.'

Julie glanced at Pierre.

'What happened?' Julie probed gently.

He shook his head and lowered his lids as if he did not want her to read the expression in his eyes. Absent-mindedly, he walked away from her and picked up a photograph from one of the side tables. He stood studying it for a moment. All traces of the flirtatious self-assured surgeon were gone. In its place stood a man who looked as if his heart had been broken. The loss of his brother and sister-in- law had obviously devastated him.

'A plane crash. My brother was piloting the plane. They'd been to France to visit me and were returning home. The weather changed suddenly but, even so, no one knows exactly what caused the accident.' He looked into the distance, his eyes bleak.

'May I?' Julie took the photograph from his unresisting fingers. It was a close-up of a woman in her early thirties and a man a few years older. Pierre's brother was smiling down at the woman as if she held the secret to his universe. In turn the woman was gazing up at her companion with unabashed adoration. Immediately Julie could see the resemblance to Caroline in the straight, aquiline nose, high cheekbones and wide mouth.

'I can see Caroline has inherited her looks from both her parents. They were an extraordinarily beautiful couple,' she said softly. 'Caroline must have been heart-broken,' Julie continued. 'To lose both, not just one parent. And so suddenly.'

'Yes, Caroline, she is in pain, I know that,' he said bleakly. 'I wish there was something I could do to help her. Sometimes it hurts me to look at her. She reminds me so much of—' He broke off and removed the photograph from Julie's hands. 'As you can see, Caroline's very like both her parents. Inside, too. She has her mother's strong will and her father's *joie de vivre*. One day she will be a remarkable young woman. I only wish she wasn't so sad and angry all the time.'

'Time will help. If she's as strong as you say, she'll come out of this.'

'*Merde*, I—' Abruptly he broke off. 'Anyway, enough sadness for now,' Pierre continued, replacing the photograph on the table. 'I don't know about you, but I am starving. *Allons-y.* Let's go through to the kitchen.'

Julie could have squeezed the whole of her flat into the kitchen of Caroline's family home. An enormous professionallooking cooker dominated one side of the room and a central work station divided the rest of the room from an eating area. Evidence of Pierre's efforts lay on the chopping board and as Julie sniffed aromas of garlic and tomato, suddenly she too was ravenous.

'I thought we'd eat in here,' Pierre said, indicating the farm-sized table which had been set with silver candlesticks and off-white roses. Catching Julie's look of surprise at the rather romantic table setting, he added hastily, 'Caroline set the table. She says it's how her mother used to do it.'

Julie cringed inwardly. Obviously he wanted to make sure she wasn't under the mistaken impression that the flickering candles and flowers were for her benefit.

'Where is Caroline?' she asked.

'Upstairs. She should be down shortly. Can I get you something to drink? White wine? Red?'

'A small glass of Chardonnay would be lovely—or some other dry white. I brought some, but stick it in the fridge if there's one open already.'

As he was pouring the wine, Caroline sauntered into the room, wearing jeans that had seen better days and a T-shirt with the name of some group Julie had only vaguely heard off emblazoned on the front.

'Hi, Julie,' she said, with a sly smirk at her uncle.

'I thought you were going upstairs to change?' Pierre said disapprovingly.

'I have changed,' Caroline responded brightly, but underneath the words Julie could detect the tension between the young girl and her uncle.

'I see you're drinking wine from my father's vineyard?' Caroline said, perching herself on a barstool beside the counter and, under the frowning gaze of Pierre, pouring herself a large measure. 'It's yummy, isn't it?'

Julie nodded. It was delicious. 'Wow! I had no idea your family owned a vineyard,' Julie said. 'I wouldn't have dreamt of bringing wine if I had known…'

'It was very kind of you,' Pierre said. 'But it's like bringing bricks to Newcastle—'

'*Coals* to Newcastle,' his niece scoffed, missing the wink that Pierre threw Julie. Then Caroline dropped her head. But not before Julie had seen the sadness in her eyes.

'The wine you're drinking was one of Dad's favourites,' Caroline said, a small catch in her voice.

'Then I feel honoured to be drinking some,' Julie said.

'Oh, yes,' Caroline snapped, narrowing her eyes. 'My family is very rich. Pierre included. Didn't you know?'

'Your uncle and I hardly know each other, Caroline. Certainly not well enough for him to discuss his finances,' Julie said, trying to keep her voice light.

'Most women seem to know exactly how rich Uncle Pierre is, don't they, Uncle?' Caroline said—almost spitefully, Julie thought. 'There's certainly enough of them hanging about.'

'Well, I'm not most women,' Julie responded with a smile,

refusing to let the younger woman rattle her. So Pierre was seeing someone. More than one woman, if Caroline was to be believed. Julie found herself inexplicably disappointed. Not that she wanted anything to do with him as a man, but over the last couple of days she had come to respect him as a doctor and wanted to believe he was more than a man who toyed with people's feelings.

'Dr McKenzie—Julie—is a champion skier.' Pierre had moved on to what he clearly hoped was safer ground, but not before Julie had seen a shadow pass across his features.

'Ex-champion skier,' Julie corrected mildly.

Just when Julie was beginning to hope that Caroline's baiting of her uncle was temporarily over, the young woman turned to her uncle. 'A champion skier *and* a doctor, Uncle Pierre! How do you do it?'

'Caroline,' Julie said mildly.

At the gentle remonstration in Julie's voice Pierre's niece visibly shrank and she had the grace to look more than a little shamefaced.

'I'm sorry. I don't mean to be a pain.' Caroline took a breath. 'Please, accept my apologies. I'm really glad you were able to come tonight. I know you probably had stuff you'd rather be doing.' She turned back to her uncle. 'Julie told me she hurt her face in a skiing accident. What a bummer.' The tension drained from her face and she looked genuinely interested. 'I didn't know you were really good, though. Why did you give it up?' She threw another disdainful look her uncle's way. 'Anybody can be a doctor, but not every one can be a great skier.'

Julie took a gulp of her wine. It still pained her to talk about the accident that had ended her career. Pierre was also looking at her keenly. With similar expressions on their faces the family resemblance was obvious.

'Maybe Julie doesn't like to talk about it,' Pierre said astutely after a moment's silence. 'Shall we talk about something else? Why don't you both sit at the table and I'll serve up the first course? I hope you like mussels, Julie?'

'I love them,' Julie said, relieved that the conversation was back on safer ground. 'I know a great fishmonger on the east side of the city. He always has the freshest supply of shellfish.'

As tucked into their starter, Julie and Pierre talked a little about where the best food in the city was to be found. It seemed they both shared a passion for cooking.

Catching Caroline looking into the distance, Julie realised they had been leaving the girl out of the conversation.

'What sports do you like, Caroline?' she asked.

'Hockey. I'm in the first team. I like skiing, too, but I'm not very good at it,' she admitted. 'My skis always seem to want to go in different directions. I spend most of the time on my backside. Kind of humiliating.'

'I could take you, if you like,' Julie offered impulsively. There was a wistfulness in the girl's expression, a look of wariness and sadness that drew Julie. She would love to see her smile. Forget her sadness even for a short while.

'I would like that,' Caroline said slowly. 'But I don't think Uncle Pierre would let me. I'm sitting my finals in a month or two, and he thinks I should be spending all my free time studying.'

Pierre stood up to clear the dishes. 'I'm sure a day off would do no harm,' he said. 'If Julie is prepared to take you.' He turned to face Julie. 'But, please, don't feel you are under any obligation.'

'As a matter of fact I was just thinking it was perfect weather for skiing this weekend, and there might not be many more opportunities before spring.' Julie said. 'I go whenever I get the chance—which isn't very often. And I'd love to have some company. None of my friends ski.'

'Then I'd really like that,' Caroline said, her eyes shining. Once again Julie was struck at the way the smile seemed to light up her face, changing her from a sullen teenager to the beautiful woman Julie predicted she was destined to become.

'You could come, too,' Caroline added, looking at her uncle. Although she said the words lightly, Julie could see that her uncle's response was important. But Pierre, busy dishing up a pan of rich-smelling stew, missed the look.

'I would like to, but I have made other arrangements for this weekend,' he said. 'Another time perhaps? But you go with Julie. Have fun.'

The light went out of Caroline's eyes. Despite her overt hostility to Pierre, Julie sensed she was hurt by his response. Losing her parents like that, and so recently, the girl was obviously in need of more emotional support than her uncle was providing. Why was it, Julie thought, that some men were so frightened of emotion and emotional involvement? And it seemed that Pierre fell squarely into this category.

'I was planning to go on Friday night. Would that suit you, Caroline? It'll be fun to have you for company,' Julie said. 'I know this cosy place to stay close to the slopes. We could ski all day on Saturday and Sunday morning and drive back on Sunday evening. How about it?'

Caroline still looked hurt. She pushed herself away from the table.

'If you like,' she said flatly. 'It seems Uncle Pierre has

more important things to do with his time. If you'll excuse me, I've had enough to eat. I'll go upstairs and leave you two adults—alone.'

Pierre looked after her retreating back, clearly bemused. He raised his eyebrows at Julie who had to hide a smile at his look of astonishment.

'*Merde,*' he said. 'What is it with women? I thought she'd be pleased to get away from me for a time.'

Julie was taken aback. Okay, he was a man, but even he couldn't be so thick-skinned he didn't recognise need when he saw it.

'I think she wants to spend more time with you. But she's a teenager. They don't want people to know when they are feeling needy. She *has* just recently lost both her parents.'

'Do you think she really wants me to come?' he said slowly. 'With most women, it is easy to know what they want. But my niece?' he sighed. 'Sometimes I just don't know how to be with her.' He pulled his hand through his hair. 'I owe it to her parents to help their daughter, but sometimes I don't even know how to help myself.' The last words were said quietly, almost as if he were speaking to himself. But there was no mistaking the naked pain in his voice. Julie resisted an instinctive impulse to reach out to offer comfort, but she guessed this man wouldn't want pity. Not from her, at any rate.

'I think it's time for me to leave,' she said instead, pushing away from the table. 'I have a busy day tomorrow and a very demanding boss.' She smiled, hoping to lighten the atmosphere. The truth was that with Caroline's departure she was suddenly aware of being alone with Pierre. Every fibre of her being seemed to react to his presence. It was mortifying the way she was responding to this man. Physically, that was. There was very little she found appealing about his personality. It was obvious to Julie he was too used to getting his own way. Too used to putting his own needs first. Suddenly she felt a wave of exasperation wash over her.

'That girl needs you. She needs someone, not a stranger, to spend time with her. Can't you see how badly she is hurting?'

Pierre looked even more bemused. Bewildered and a little shocked at Julie's outburst. But no more shocked than Julie herself. How could she have forgotten? The man was her boss after all. If he wanted to, he could have her put off his team. There would be plenty of other juniors only too ready to take her place.

'I'm sorry,' Julie mumbled. 'That was rude of me and I had no right to say what I did. Now, I really should be going.'

Pierre crossed the room. For a moment he stared down at her, searching her face with silver eyes.

'It is me who should be apologising,' he said. 'You are right, and I am an idiot.' He placed a hand on Julie's shoulder and she felt a flash of heat at his touch. 'Forgive me?'

Julie felt herself sway as her knees went weak. 'It's not me whose forgiveness you should be asking,' she said. 'It's that girl up there.' She softened at the look on his face. 'Go and talk to her,' she prompted. 'Make her realise that she is important to you. That you care about her.'

'You will still take her skiing?' he asked. Despite the look of entreaty on his face, Julie told herself it was Caroline that influenced her decision.

'Yes, if she still wants to. Of course.'

'And I, I will ask Katherine and perhaps we will come, too?' He looked pleased at his inspired piece of logic.

So that was it, Julie thought, furious with the way her heart plummeted. The arrangements he had made were with another woman. Well, why not? She couldn't see a man like Pierre not having a girlfriend in tow. It was what she'd suspected all along. He was handsome, successful and rich. He was bound to have his pick of women.

'I think, if you are going to come along, you should leave your girlfriend behind,' she said softly. Then she blushed. What if he thought that she wanted him all to herself? Well, she would soon disabuse him of that notion. 'Caroline needs you to spend time with her away from other *distractions*,' she added pointedly, remembering his comment the day she had first met him.

He raised an eyebrow. 'Touché,' he said. 'I can't see Katherine wanting to spend the day in the freezing cold anyway. She is a woman who likes her comforts.'

Although Julie had never met this Katherine and was unlikely to do so, she suspected she would hate her on sight.

'Now that is settled,' he continued. 'Let's finish dinner and then we can talk about work.'

Julie could tell he was determined she eat the stew he had dished up. And furthermore she didn't want to miss the opportunity to talk over the coming week's cases with him. At least they'd be on safe territory. She relaxed and dipped her bread into the bowl of stew.

'Tell me, why plastic surgery?' she asked. 'And what about that technique you're teaching us at the hospital? What is so special about it?'

CHAPTER FOUR

THE next couple of days flew past. Julie found plastic surgery fascinating. Every day there was something new to learn and she found she had little time for anything except work and reading up on the following day's cases. The more she saw of the way Pierre operated the more impressed she became with his surgical skills.

Most days Pierre's team barely stopped for coffee, let alone lunch, but Julie didn't mind. She was working at a job she loved, with a man who, professionally at least, she admired increasingly.

With the weekend looming and no confirmation from either Caroline or her uncle about the trip to the Cairngorms, Julie wondered if she should give the teenager a call. She didn't want to ask Pierre in case it put him on the spot. She was mulling over the dilemma when he unexpectedly plonked himself down at her table in the canteen where she was having a solitary lunch.

'I hear the snow up north is *perfect* for skiing,' he said, wrapping some pasta around his fork. 'So does that mean you are still going and Caroline and I are still invited? I'll understand if you want to go alone, have quiet time—it's been crazy here—*non*?'

Julie's heart thudded treacherously. Outside Theatre or the wards, she felt awkward in Pierre's presence. If she hadn't promised Caroline, she would have found a way to call the whole thing off.

'I checked with the bed-and-breakfast place I normally use,' she said slowly. 'They do have a couple of rooms available this weekend. Caroline and I could share. But wouldn't you prefer to stay in a hotel?'

'Why? Is there something about this place you are not telling me?'

'I just thought you'd prefer something a little more luxurious,' Julie said. 'I love this place, but it's cosy rather than fancy.'

Pierre raised an eyebrow, a small smile playing at the corners of his mouth. 'And you think I wouldn't like it. Why?'

'I—I don't know. It's just…' Julie stammered. 'You strike me as the kind of man who usually stays in five-star hotels rather than small bed and breakfasts.'

He leaned back in his chair. 'You know all about me, then?' Julie wasn't sure—was he teasing her?

'No, of course I don't know anything about you except you are a great surgeon.' She blushed. She hadn't meant to say that. It had just slipped out. Now she sounded like some star-struck teenager.

'I am delighted you approve of my surgical skills,' he said. 'But I can assure you I am happy to stay anywhere. I draw the line at camping, but only because it's snowing—and I'm sure Caroline won't go anywhere she won't be able to use her hair gadgets and all that other stuff you women seem to need to get ready in the morning.'

'I don't need stuff like that!' Julie protested, before catching sight of his grin and realising that he really was teasing her.

'Anyway,' she added, 'I know more than one man who spends just as much time in the bathroom as some women.'

'Really and who are these men? Boyfriends?'

'No,' Julie said, more sharply than she'd intended. She changed the subject. 'If you're happy with my choice of accommodation then I'll confirm it later today when I get a chance. We should plan to leave as soon as possible after work on Friday.'

Pierre stood, stretching his lean frame. '*D'accord*. It is settled. We'll pick you up at your flat. In the meantime, we need to get down to Theatre. Our first patient should be about to arrive.'

Julie stood, too. 'The breast reconstruction following a double mastectomy?' she said. 'Mrs Simpson?' She almost had to run to keep up with his long strides. 'Her husband is more scared about the operation than she is,' she said. 'I really hope everything goes well for them.' Pierre stopped so suddenly Julie almost collided with him.

'Don't you know by now, Dr McKenzie? Everything I do goes well.'

Julie almost spluttered at his arrogance. But, then again, who would she rather have operating on her? A man who doubted his skills or the man in front of her who seemed to have no doubts at all—about anything?

Before leaving work on Friday, Julie went to check up on Tom. As usual, she found Trudi sitting beside his bed. She looked up from the book she was reading to Tom when she spotted Julie.

'Look, Tom, it's our favourite doctor come to see you.' Although the tube had been removed from Tom's throat a few days before, he still couldn't speak. It would be another few days before he would be able to. However, he smiled to let Julie know he was pleased to see her.

'How are you doing, guys?' Julie said, picking up a magazine from the top of the bedcover. 'Hey, what's this? *The Bride*?'

'We're getting married,' Trudi said, her eyes shining. 'We had always planned to eventually. But now it seems crazy to wait. We're planning for June—do you think that will be enough time for Tom to be fit? And we want you and Dr Favatier to be our guests of honour.'

Julie felt her throat constrict. Trudi and Tom were both so brave. They obviously loved each other deeply. She looked away, blinking back tears. Seeing Trudi brought back memories of Luke. Her parents had told her that he had spent the first few days after the accident refusing to leave her bedside, although she had no memory of it. By the time she'd come round, a couple of weeks later, he had no longer been there. At first her parents had told her that he'd had to leave to compete in a downhill race in Europe. Later, when she'd been stronger, they'd admitted that his visits had simply tailed off, until one day he hadn't come back. When she'd realised Luke had gone for good, she had sobbed her heart out. But then, once she had cried herself out, she had promised herself she would never again allow a man to make her shed a single tear. She had heard that Luke had carried on skiing, winning a bronze in the Commonwealth Games, and had become engaged to another girl in the British team shortly afterwards. She had thought it would hurt, but it hadn't. And, true to her promise to herself, she had never let another man get close to her. These days she had her work, and it meant everything to her. She didn't need a man to make her feel complete.

Trudi was looking at her expectantly. Julie realised she was still waiting for an answer.

'Of course I'd love to come to your wedding,' she said. Instinctively she knew that Trudi loved Tom enough to cope with whatever the consequences of Tom's injuries might be. Whatever he would look like on the outside was immaterial to Trudi. Julie doubted if she'd even notice the scars.

'And your boyfriend, Dr Favatier, you think he'll come, too?'

'What on earth makes you think he's my boyfriend?' Julie spluttered.

'You were both at the nightclub that night. I just assumed… And the way you look at him. Oh, dear,' Trudi finished limply. 'I've put my foot it in, haven't I? Tom's always telling me I don't think before I speak, aren't you, honey?'

Julie felt her cheeks blaze. What did Trudi mean? How *did* she look at Pierre?

'Dr Favatier's my boss,' she said quietly. 'Nothing more.'

'Of course. I'm sorry…' Trudi stumbled. 'Please forget I said anything.'

'Don't worry about it,' Julie said. 'I suppose it was an easy mistake to make once you knew we were both at the nightclub. But we were there separately, for different reasons.' She knew she was babbling, but couldn't help herself. She kept thinking of Trudi's words. Good God, did other people think the same thing? What about Pierre? What did he think? It was too embarrassing for words. If it had been possible, Julie would have avoided Pierre for the rest of her life. As it was she was going away with him for the weekend. She suppressed a groan. Why had Dr Pierre Favatier come into her life now? Why couldn't he have stayed in France and left her life the way she liked it? Calm, uneventful, and—she admitted reluctantly—ever so slightly boring.

By the time Julie arrived home, she only had enough time to take a quick shower and throw a few things into an overnight bag. She jumped when she heard the doorbell. After what Trudi had said, she wanted more than ever to cancel the trip, but, short of being admitted to hospital herself, she knew there was nothing else that would justify cancelling at such short notice.

She answered the door still in her bathrobe, her hair wrapped in a towel.

'Not quite ready, then?' Pierre asked, striding into her flat before Julie had time to suggest he wait for her in the car. His powerful frame seemed to dwarf her tiny sitting room. Hastily Julie shoved her cat, Toto, off the armchair and onto the floor, where he landed with a squeal of protest.

'Please, take a seat,' she offered. 'I won't be long.' She peered past Pierre to the door. 'Where's Caroline?'

Pierre sat down, reaching down to stroke Toto, who immediately sprang into his lap. Julie was surprised. Toto didn't like strangers. She had rescued him as a kitten and he barely tolerated anyone besides Julie. Even Kim, who fed him when Julie was away, had experienced the odd scratch.

'She's in the car. Listening to her MP3 player.' Pierre said. Toto stretched luxuriously as Pierre looked around. 'I like your flat. It's exactly how I expected it to be.'

Julie glanced around her home with its mish-mash of furniture and objects she had collected from her travels around the world. She loved it, especially in the winter when she would light the gas fire, draw the curtains against the winter weather and curl up on her old but comfortable sofa with a good book. But somehow she didn't think it was Pierre's style. She imagined him more minimalist. All sleek lines and no clutter. And what did he mean, it was how he'd expected it to be? Was he suggesting she wasn't cool and sophisticated? Well, in that respect at least he was right. She wasn't and would never be.

'Thank you,' she said simply, retreating into her bedroom. 'I'll be as quick as I can.'

By the time she returned five minutes later dressed in jeans and a black polo neck with her still damp hair tied in a braid, Pierre seemed to have dozed off. For a moment she stood looking down at him, taking in the thick lashes hiding his sharp blue eyes and his long legs stretched out in front of him. Toto was still curled up in his lap, purring contentedly. Asleep, Pierre looked almost human, she thought. He must be exhausted. She had seen first hand how hard he worked. When he wasn't on the wards or operating she had heard him tell one of the other doctors that he was writing up some research for a paper in a leading medical journal.

As she reached forward to shake him awake, his eyes opened. For a second he looked dazed.

'Iona,' he said, so softly Julie wasn't sure she had heard him correctly. He reached out and trailed long fingers along her arm. Then he seemed to come to. A flicker of terrible sadness crossed his features and he let his arm drop to his side before struggling to his feet. Toto jumped off his lap with a meow of protest.

'*Bon*,' Pierre said shortly. 'You are ready to go?'

Julie thought she must have imagined the look on his face. His eyes were hooded and his mouth in a straight line. He seemed almost brusque as he picked up her overnight bag and headed for the door. Had she imagined that he had said his sister-in-law's name? Why would he have had Iona's name on his lips? And why that awful look of loss? Had there been more to his relationship with his brother's wife than anyone knew? Julie shivered. No, she was jumping to conclusions. Whatever she thought of him, she had never imagined him the kind of man to have an affair with his brother's wife. But it *would* explain why Caroline was so antagonistic towards him. She pushed the unsettling images from her mind. What on earth was she doing? Allowing herself to get caught up in the messy lives of these two wounded people? Hadn't she promised herself that she would never get too involved again?

The journey to the Cairngorms passed quickly. Pierre had hired a four-wheel-drive for the journey north, a wise decision as it turned out as the roads were almost obscured by the falling snow. His sports car would never have made it. As it was, the conditions required Pierre's full concentration and as Caroline was still plugged into her music, Julie was left to her own thoughts as they progressed northwards. Despite her best efforts they kept returning to the comment Trudi had made about the way she looked at Pierre. Whatever happened over the next day and a half, she needed to ensure that Pierre didn't make the same *incorrect* assumption.

'The landlady said she'd keep us some supper,' she said. 'She knows we might be held up.'

'Good,' said Pierre. 'I didn't have time to eat earlier. And neither did Caroline, I'm sure.'

'It won't be much. Just sandwiches and a flask of coffee, I suspect.'

'Is there a restaurant near by?' Pierre asked. 'Where we could get something more substantial?'

'No, the place where we will be staying is pretty remote,' Julie apologised. 'I did warn you it might not be what you're used to. Besides, I didn't think we'd need anything more than a snack.'

'Sandwiches will be fine, as long as there's somewhere we can get a drink,' came Caroline's voice from the back seat.

Julie glanced at Pierre. In the light from the dashboard she could see that he was annoyed.

'Back with us?' Julie asked, turning around in her seat to address Caroline. Pierre's niece had removed her earphones.

'I don't think we should be concerning ourselves with getting a drink,' he said sourly. 'As long as there is something to eat, it'll be just about time for bed.'

Out of sight, Caroline stuck a tongue out at her uncle's back. Julie suppressed the desire to giggle. He did sound a little pompous. Still, she wondered at the girl's blatant desire to needle her uncle. And his reaction to his niece was equally strange. Sometimes it was as if he could hardly bear to be in the young girl's company. And if Julie sensed that, surely so would Caroline.

'It's the weekend and I am almost eighteen, Pierre,' Caroline said. 'I wish you would stop treating me like a child. Soon I'll be able to live on my own.'

'But you're not eighteen yet,' Pierre said quietly, 'and until you are, it was your parents' wish that I look after you. And one way or another, that's what I'm going to do.'

'You know Pierre stole my father's inheritance?' Caroline burst out bitterly.

Pierre's expression was thunderous.

'You know that's not correct. Anyway, I don't think Julie is interested in our family business, Caroline.'

Julie was curious. What was going on between these two? Instinctively she knew Pierre wasn't the kind of man who would take something that didn't belong to him. Well, not material things anyway. She wasn't too sure about women. But he was right. It was none of her business. The awkward moment was broken as they drew up in front of their accommodation. They were barely out of the car before Mrs Fletcher, the landlady, was at the door.

'Come away in.' She gesticulated. 'It's a bitter night.'

Julie went over to her and kissed her cheek. 'Doris, it's lovely to see you again,' she said.

'And you, pet. But let's not stand here. Let's get you inside. I've a fire on in the sitting room. You must be hungry after your journey. Leave your bags in the hall. Johnny will take them up for you.'

Pierre looked bemused as Doris, still chatting ninety to the dozen, took their coats and ushered them into the sitting room. True to her word there was a blazing fire in the grate, and in front of the fire a coffee-table groaning with sandwiches and home baking.

'You shouldn't have gone to all this trouble, Doris,' Julie protested, even as her stomach grumbled in anticipation.

'I know you doctors don't get time to eat properly, and you'll need your strength for skiing tomorrow,' Doris said, hovering over them.

'It looks delicious,' Pierre replied, looking at the spread hungrily.

As they warmed themselves by the fire, Julie made the introductions. Doris eyed Pierre with interest.

'A Frenchman, are you?' Doris said. 'I'm afraid I have nothing fancy. I know how you French like your food.'

Julie and Pierre exchanged glances and Julie had to bite down on her lip to stop herself laughing out loud. She had known Doris for years and was well used to her ways, but suddenly she could see that to a stranger, she might appear curt—rude even.

'I'm sure everything will be delicious,' Julie said as soon as Doris stopped for breath. 'On my part anything that doesn't come from a hospital canteen has a head start.' As Doris frowned, Julie added hastily, 'Not that your food bears the remotest resemblance to anything from the hospital dining room.'

Doris appeared reassured. 'Well, sit yourself down while I fetch soup. That little one doesn't look as if she's had a proper meal in days,' she added disapprovingly, taking in Caroline's slender frame. 'Indeed, she looks as if she'll just snap in the wind. The soup's cock-a-leekie, by the way—a Scottish specialty.' With a brief challenging look at Pierre, she hurried out of the room. Catching Caroline's expression of astonishment and chagrin, Julie could no longer hold back her laughter. Soon they were all laughing, trying desperately to smother the sound before it reached Doris's ears.

'She is quite a character, your Doris,' Pierre remarked before wolfing down a sandwich.

'Was she suggesting I was too thin?' a smiling Caroline added. 'Just wait till I tell my friends. They are always telling me I should lose weight.'

'I hope you don't pay them any attention,' Pierre said, his features becoming sombre once again. 'You barely eat enough as it is.'

This time it was Caroline and Julie who exchanged looks. Increasingly Julie was feeling caught in the middle.

'Men don't understand these things,' Julie offered. 'C'mon, let's get stuck in, and then,' she added, noting Caroline's yawn, 'I'm for bed.'

After finishing their supper under the watchful eye of Doris, who was somewhat mollified when Pierre insisted on having two helpings of her clootie dumpling, protesting it was the best he had ever had. Julie suspected he had never had any before, so even if it hadn't been up to Doris's usual standards, he was still telling the truth.

Doris had managed to find them a bedroom each as there were no other guests. Caroline and Pierre had politely insisted that Julie take the larger double while they each took one of the singles. As Julie sank into the bed, pulling the feather quilt up to her chin, she wondered why, for the first time in as long as she could remember, she felt happy. Even as she told herself it was the combination of good food and a soft bed, along with the prospect of a day's skiing on new snow, she knew she was kidding herself. Being in Pierre and Caroline's company felt good. It was almost as if they were a family. As soon as she had the thought, she dismissed it. She would do well to remember the reasons for this trip. Any daydreams she might have belonged just there. In her dreams.

Following an enormous breakfast from Doris, they found themselves at the foot of the mountains before nine the next morning. The snow was still falling gently, but the wind had died down. The sky was blue and the sun shone. It was a perfect day for skiing, Julie thought happily, although, as she eyed darker clouds to the west, she wondered if the weather would hold.

They had discussed their plans over breakfast and agreed

that Julie would give Caroline some private tuition in the morning while Pierre skied higher up. After lunch, if the weather held, the two of them would take Caroline down some of the gentler red runs.

'I don't think there's much chance of that,' Caroline had said nervously. 'If my skiing is as good as the last time I tried, then it'll be the green runs all day for me.'

'Let's just wait and see,' Julie said soothingly. 'Don't worry, I won't make you do anything you're not ready for.'

They waved Pierre off and, after getting Caroline fitted with some skis and boots, they headed onto the nursery slopes. At first Caroline kept falling down, but under Julie's careful tutoring she gained in confidence. Soon she was ready to try the tow bar to the higher runs.

Julie hid her amusement as Caroline landed in a heap several times before successfully managing to hold on long enough to reach the top. She knew it was unfair for her to laugh. Just because she couldn't remember a time when she couldn't ski, just as she couldn't remember a time when she couldn't walk, it didn't mean she wasn't impressed at the younger woman's determination and resolve. She was beginning to see that Caroline was more like Pierre than either of them wanted to acknowledge.

After a few runs, Caroline was even beginning to get to grips with parallel turns. Julie could tell it wouldn't be long before she could manage the trickier red runs. Not wanting to exhaust her pupil, she thought it would be best if they stopped for a bit.

As they stood at the top of the gentle slope, preparing to descend, Julie turned to her companion.

'Didn't your parents ski?' she asked. 'Pierre said he'd been skiing since he was very young. That must have been true of your father, too?'

'Oh, yes,' Caroline agreed. 'Papa was a great skier. Not as good as Pierre, but almost. Mum said they were always really competitive. Apparently he and Pierre used to go to the mountains every time they got the opportunity and race each other.'

'Didn't he teach you, then? He must have taken you in Scotland sometimes?'

'My mother hated skiing,' Caroline said. 'She thought Papa was too reckless and wouldn't let him take me. She said she had once watched Pierre and Papa skiing together and it had scared her out of her wits. Papa told her he'd never take risks with me, but she wouldn't take the chance. I think he was disappointed I never really learned. I think there were many things about me that disappointed him.'

'Oh, no, Caroline, I'm sure you're wrong. I suspect your dad was very proud of you. You're a beautiful, bright girl who shows a lot of courage.'

'How can you say that? You hardly know me! Anyway, it's easy for you to say. You've been successful at everything. I bet your parents were really proud of you.'

'They weren't always proud,' Julie said quietly. She thought for a moment, remembering the weeks after the accident. 'Look…' She pointed to a hut a few metres down the slope. 'There's a restaurant down there. Let's stop for a hot chocolate and then we can talk properly.'

'Good idea,' Caroline agreed enthusiastically. 'I could do with a rest. My thighs feel as if I've run a marathon! Not that I'd know what that feels like.' She grinned at Julie, before setting off tentatively in the direction of the hut.

Julie skied in front of her, indicating that the girl follow her path. That way she could ensure that Caroline took the easiest route.

As they stopped in front of the café, Caroline was smiling. Her cheeks were flushed and her eyes sparkling. 'Hey,' she said 'I really think I'm getting the hang of this. You make it seem so easy. I don't know why I found it so impossible before.'

As the two women settled themselves at a table with their steaming mugs of hot chocolate, Julie picked up the conversation where they had left off. She was becoming very fond of Caroline and she wanted her to know that she too had had to struggle with demons.

'After the accident, when I knew that I would never ski competitively again, I reacted badly. I guess I was angry. My dreams had been taken from me, and then my boyfriend left. When I first looked in the mirror—when they finally let me— I cried for days.' Caroline was looking at her with interest. Julie shifted in her seat, taking another gulp from her mug.

'I thought no one would ever want me again. And with my skiing career over I believed there was nothing left for me. No future.' She paused and looked over Caroline's shoulder out onto the hills. She hated remembering those dark days and how she had pushed her family and friends away. She still felt ashamed.

'I suppose you could say I went off the rails a bit. Not in the way most teenagers do. If I hadn't felt so self-conscious about the way I looked, I probably would have hit the bars and nightclubs. Instead, I stayed in my room, refusing to see anyone. Not even my best friends.' She laughed bitterly at the memory. 'They tried to get me to go out with them, but I refused even to see them. Eventually they stopped calling. My parents would beg me to come out of my room, to go out with my friends, if not with them, but I wouldn't. I'm ashamed to ay I took all my anger out on my folks. They really had a ough time.'

'What happened then?' Caroline asked. Julie could see that the teenager was identifying with her story.

'Up in my room, I began to get bored. It's kind of exhausting, thinking of yourself all of the time.' She smiled ruefully. My parents made me see I needed to focus my energy somewhere. So I threw myself into my school work. Skiing and ravelling around the world hadn't left much time for studying. Although I had always managed to pass my exams, I had never xcelled. And my time in hospital made me very interested in medicine.' She finished her drink. Caroline was still hanging nto every word. 'I thought to myself that if skiing was over, needed another career, and maybe medicine was the one. I tudied like mad and…well, I guess the rest is history.'

'I haven't been doing very well at school lately,' Caroline dmitted. 'I just can't get myself to care. And I can't get myself to want to see my friends. Sometimes I feel so jealous f them. They still have their parents.'

'It's only natural to feel the way you do. You've suffered terrible, shocking loss, and it will take time for life to seem etter again.'

'I don't think it ever will.' Caroline's voice broke. 'I think 'm going to feel like this for the rest of my life.' Her eyes himmered and Julie's heart went out to her. She reached ver and took her hand. 'It will get better, I promise you. 'ou'll always miss your parents, but in time you'll be able to aink of them without experiencing the dreadful pain you're eeling now.'

'What happened to your mother and father?' Caroline asked.

'My folks were older than most by the time they had me,'

Julie said thoughtfully. 'Mum said they had resigned themselves to not having children—then I came along.'

'They must have been thrilled,' Caroline said.

'They were. But, you know, in a weird way I think they had got used to just being the two of them—and I was away so much as a child because of the skiing.' She hesitated. 'To be honest, I never felt truly part of the family. They were so wrapped up in each other. At times I felt like an outsider.'

Caroline looked sympathetic. 'I always knew my parents adored me,' she said. 'Even knowing they loved each other terribly.' Her voice cracked.

'Oh, I knew mine loved me,' Julie said. 'But I think they loved each other more. Then, just over a year ago, my mother was diagnosed with breast cancer. It had already spread to her liver and she died a few months later.' This time it was Julie's voice that cracked. 'After she died, Dad was so lost. Nothing I could do or say seemed to make a difference. Then two months after Mum, he died too. Then I was truly on my own.'

'I'm sorry,' Caroline said simply. She bit her lip and a tear slid down her cheek. 'When Uncle Pierre said he was coming to Scotland, at first I was glad. At least I wouldn't be on my own. But now that he's here, sometimes I think he hates me.'

'Oh, no, Caroline, I'm sure you're mistaken. You're his niece. His brother's child.'

'Sometimes,' Caroline went on, as if Julie hadn't spoken, 'it's as if he can't bear the sight of me. Almost as if he's angry with me and wishes he was as far away from me as possible—back in France. I don't know why he just doesn't go and leave me. Anyway, it's me that should be angry with him. If he had come to Scotland instead of making them go to France, they'd still be alive.'

Julie reached for Caroline's hand and grasped it firmly. 'He doesn't hate you,' she said. 'Maybe he too is suffering…' She broke off as Caroline's eyes fixed on something over her shoulder. Once again it was as if the shutters had come down. Her mouth regained its sullen downturn and her eyes became flat. Julie swivelled round in her chair to find Pierre standing over them.

'I saw you coming in here as I was going up in the lift.' He sat down beside them, stretching his long legs in front of him, apparently oblivious to the tension in the air. 'The wind is getting up a bit at the top—I'm not sure how much longer we'll be able to ski.' He leaned back in his chair, looking relaxed.

'Why don't you two go on?' Caroline said. 'I think I'd like to rest.'

'We could all go up together—you could show your uncle how much progress you've made this morning.' Julie suggested. She slid a look at Pierre, urging him with her eyes to join her in her encouraging Caroline.

'I'd like that,' he said simply.

'We could go up to the top,' Julie suggested. 'There are gentle red runs with only one steepish bit that would take us all the way down to the car park. It'll take us about an hour. It's where I take my kids.'

Pierre looked at her curiously. 'Kids? You have children?' he said, looking shocked.

Julie laughed and then explained about Richard. 'When he was going through a period of remission, he persuaded me to take him to the dry slope just outside Edinburgh and give him and a group of his friends some skiing lessons. Ever since then I take them away occasionally for skiing on real snow—when there is some, that is.'

'That's who you were with the night of the fire?' Caroline asked.

'Yes.' Julie smiled. 'They insisted I go with them. They said they had to do what I said most of the time, so I should do as they ask at least some of the time. It was Richard's birthday, so I could hardly refuse although nightclubs aren't really my scene.'

Pierre was looking at her intently. There was something in his expression that made her feel warm inside.

'You should come and meet them some time, Caroline,' she added.

'Why don't you, Caroline?' Pierre said. 'It might help.'

Caroline stood, fastening her ski jacket. 'I don't think I need to hang out with a bunch of kids,' she said dismissively. 'Come on, if we are going up, let's go.'

Pierre and Julie exchanged glances. She could tell from his puzzled, almost hurt look that he didn't know what he had said wrong. She wiggled an eyebrow at him, warning him not to say any more.

The descent from the top of the hill took, as Julie had estimated, just over an hour. She skied backwards down the difficult parts of the slope, guiding Caroline while praising her efforts. Pierre, watching Julie ski, copied her. Grinning wickedly, Julie suspected he was challenging her to a backwards race, and laughed.

'Let's wait until we get Caroline safely down, then I'll take you up to the Five Finger Gully. We can race from there. See if you are as good a skier as you say.'

'You may be a good skier, a great skier, in fact, but you are still only a girl,' he threw back at her.

So he was throwing down the gauntlet, Julie thought. Well, they would see. There was no way he was going to beat her in a race. She felt the familiar surge of adrenaline she always got when she was about to challenge herself. She was looking forward to wiping that smug grin off his face. Pierre spun round on his skis and headed off to the side. He found a series of bumps of snow, moguls, and schussed over them. Taking her eyes off Caroline, she watched him for a few moments, marvelling at the way a man of his size could look so elegant on skis. When she turned back to Caroline, the girl seemed to have found her rhythm and was heading in a straightish line down the slope. Just as Julie caught up with her, Caroline wobbled and, shrieking, collided with Julie, spilling them both in a tumbled heap. By the time Julie had untangled her skis from Caroline's they were both in a fit of giggles.

'Hey, I fell,' Caroline gasped. 'And I'm okay! And you fell too!'

'I fall often enough,' Julie admitted. 'It's all part of skiing.' She looked up as a shadow fell across them. Pierre was looking down at them. He too was smiling.

'Are you both okay?' he asked. 'And I thought you were an expert!' Julie and Caroline looked at each other, then almost in unison they each picked up a handful of snow. Taking aim, they threw their snowballs at Pierre. Both scored direct hits—Caroline to his shoulder, Julie to his forehead. Within seconds they had a full-scale snowball fight as Pierre retaliated.

After taking a few hits, Julie held up her hands in surrender. 'Enough,' she gasped. 'It feels as if I've half the mountain down my back.'

'You admit defeat?' Pierre asked with a glint in his eye.

Julie nodded. *'Et tu, petite?'* he asked his niece. At her nod of confirmation, he held out his hands to the two women. 'Let me help you up.' Once again there was no need for words between Caroline and Julie. They let Pierre pull them halfway up then, when he was most off balance they fell back, pulling him onto the snow. Within seconds Caroline had pinned him down while Julie heaped snow down his jacket. This time it was Pierre who begged them to stop.

'Okay. You win,' he said. As Caroline got to her feet, he pulled Julie towards him. Losing her balance, she fell onto his chest. For a moment it felt to Julie as if the earth had stopped spinning on its axis. She looked into Pierre's silver eyes. She was so close she could see her reflection in them. Even through the combined softness of their ski gear she was aware of the hard muscles of his body along her length. She felt a shiver of desire so strong it almost took her breath away. Flustered by her feelings and conscious of Caroline in the background, Julie extricated herself. Her heart was thumping in her chest and she could feel the heat in her cheeks.

'We'd better get going,' she said abruptly. 'If we are going to have a last run after we leave Caroline.' Caroline was replacing her skis. She looks happy, Julie thought. For once she looks how a girl of her age having fun should look like.

'Yeah, I need some food,' Caroline groaned. 'I'm not used to all this exercise.'

After Pierre and Julie deposited Caroline back at the foot of the mountain, they caught the ski lift back up for the final run of the day. The clouds were darkening, and Julie suspected there was another fall of snow on the way. Going up on the chair lift, she was very conscious of Pierre next to her. She couldn't remember when she had last had so much fun. She touched her cheek. She had even forgotten about her scar.

'Thank you,' Pierre said, breaking into her thoughts.

'What for?'

'For letting us take up your precious spare time. You are, I see, a woman who is generous with herself. I haven't seen Caroline looking so happy since…' He tailed off.

'She just needs time,' Julie said. 'She's a strong-willed girl. I'm sure she'll come through it.'

'All the same, if it wasn't for your efforts, I suspect she'd still be holed up in that room of hers, trying to avoid me at every opportunity.'

'She needs time to get to know you. You'll just have to be patient with her.'

Pierre looked grim. 'I hope it will be as simple as you say, but…'

Julie looked at him expectantly, waiting for him to go on.

'I think she blames me for the loss of her parents,' he said eventually. From the way he spoke the words, Julie could tell he wasn't a man who was used to talking about emotions.

'Why would she do that? Surely it had nothing to do with you?'

The chair lift was approaching the top of the mountain. Pierre lifted the safety bar in preparation for their arrival.

'That's where you're wrong,' he said. 'In a way she is right. I am responsible.' But before Julie could ask him what he meant, it was time for them to ski off the lift.

CHAPTER FIVE

JULIE and Pierre raced down the black run. He wasn't a bad skier at all, she had to admit. Still, she knew she could ski faster if she needed to. She'd let him think he was giving a run for her money—then she'd show him.

They sped on down the slope, hitting a series of moguls. Julie bent her knees, absorbing the bumps and hardly slowing down. At the last moment Pierre shot past her, using a bigger bump on the slope to lift him into the air. To her dismay, it was enough to put him in the lead for the first time. He looked back at her, grinning widely in triumph. Let him enjoy his moment, Julie thought. Little did he know it wasn't going to last. She waited until the perfect opportunity presented itself. A few moments later they came to the narrowest bit of the run. To the side, the snow was banked and Julie used the rise to pass Pierre before he knew what was happening. This time it was her who flashed him a grin of triumph. She crouched low, feeling the familiar surge of excitement as she allowed herself to go with the speed. Looking round, she saw that she was leaving Pierre behind. 'Hah!' she muttered under her breath. 'That'll teach you to underestimate a woman.'

She had removed her skis and was standing, watching, when Pierre skidded to a stop beside her.

'Show-off,' he said, but he was laughing. 'I knew that you could ski, but I have never seen anything like it. Have you no fear, woman?'

'Just enough to keep me safe,' she said. 'Anyway you're not too bad yourself. The only man I've met who can give me a run for my money.'

She took a sharp intake of breath. That hadn't come out exactly the way she had meant it to.

'I can't imagine there are many men who could give you "a run for your money", as you say,' he said with a wicked glint in his eye, 'but I would like to try some time.'

Julie felt her heart thump. There was something in the way he was looking at her that made her breath catch in her throat. But as soon as the thought entered her mind she dismissed it. It was more likely that he saw her as one of the boys. Or a friend for his niece. His words couldn't mean anything else, *could they*?

Not knowing what else to do, she looked around for Caroline, but couldn't see her anywhere. The snow had begun to fall in earnest and it looked as if most people were leaving. The car park only had a few vehicles left. Pierre's niece was probably sheltering indoors, but when she looked inside the restaurant Caroline was nowhere to be seen. In the meantime, Pierre had gone to check the car. But apparently Caroline wasn't there either.

'Where is she?' Pierre said. 'We should get on our way.'

Suddenly a thought struck Julie. She remembered their conversation from earlier about wanting to show her uncle what she was made of. And she had been so delighted with the progress she had made under Julie's tuition. It wasn't possible that she had gone up the slopes for one last run on her own. Was it?

It seemed as if Pierre was having the same thoughts. All the humour had left his face as he marched up to the gondola they had used earlier to access the middle runs. The operator was packing up for the day, the lift having completed its final run. Julie, scurrying after him, was only just in time to hear the operator's response. 'Yes, a young woman in a red ski jacket went up half an hour ago. I told her that it would have to be her last run and she needed to make it quick, but she went anyway. What's up? Has she not come back down?'

Pierre swore, a long stream of French that Julie was almost thankful she couldn't follow. She scanned the mountain. There were still a few stragglers coming down. Julie knew that staff would be skiing the slopes ensuring that no one was left on the mountain. If Caroline had got into difficulty, they would come across her—she hoped.

'I'm going back up to look for her,' Pierre said. Julie could see he was desperately worried.

'You can't go back up. They won't let you. Not at this time. Besides, the lifts are closed.'

Pierre swung back to face her. For a moment she almost recoiled from the look in his eyes. He looked furious.

'I will not let anything happen to Iona's daughter.'

Surely he meant Jacques and Iona's daughter? Julie thought. Wouldn't it be more usual for him to think of her as his brother's daughter?

'They will find her,' Julie said. But her words fell in the wind as Pierre strode off towards the main office area. Somehow Julie suspected that he would get his way. But before he reached the office Julie spotted the red jacket and brightly coloured hat belonging to Caroline. She came to a controlled halt at the bottom of the slope, almost directly in front of Pierre. As Caroline removed her hat and goggles, Julie could see she was smiling broadly. Thank God, Julie thought, heading in the direction of Pierre and his niece.

Even from a distance she could hear Pierre berating his niece in French. Caroline's smile had vanished, in its place the more familiar sulky look. Pierre came to an end of his tirade just as Julie reached the pair.

'Nice to see you,' Julie said neutrally.

'I don't know why he…' Caroline cast a disdainful look at her uncle '…is making such a fuss. I'm perfectly all right. I just thought I'd go up one more time by myself. Just to see if I could do it.'

'I've said what I had to say, now we'd better be on our way.' He turned on his heel and headed back towards the car.

'Typical!' Caroline said. 'Nothing I do is ever right. I thought he'd be pleased that I managed on my own.'

'He was worried about you. We both were. It's getting dark and, as you can see, the snow is really heavy now. We really need to get on our way, before it gets worse.' Julie looked around. Needles of snow bounced off the ground. As the sun left the sky, the temperature was dropping. Tonight, Julie knew, it would be well below freezing.

'For God's sake,' Caroline said. 'Would the pair of you stop treating me like a child!'

Julie had to smile at Caroline's furious expression. If only she knew how young she looked right at that moment.

'I'm sorry,' she said. 'You're quite right.' She changed the subject as they trudged towards the car. 'Well done, by the way. Who would have thought this morning that a few hours later you'd be off on your own? Next time we'll try the harder red runs.'

'It was great. I loved it. Every minute. Well, almost…' She glared at her uncle's back. Thankfully he didn't catch the look as he was changing out of his ski boots. 'I am sorry that we have to leave earlier than expected, but thank you for inviting me.'

'You are welcome.' Julie replied. 'And we'll do it again if there's more snow before spring.' So much for bringing Caroline and Pierre closer together, Julie thought ruefully. Now it seemed they were back where they had started, circling each other like two wary tigers. What on earth was really going on between them?

The journey back to Edinburgh that night was a subdued affair. Once again Caroline plugged herself into her headphones, making it clear she had no wish to speak to her uncle. The snow was falling so heavily it made driving even more difficult than on the way up. Julie knew they had left just in time—they were bound to close the road behind them soon. She switched on the radio, finding the classical music station she preferred, and let the music wash over her. Sliding a glance at the man seated beside her, she could barely recall the laughing man of the snow fight.

He must have felt her eyes on him as he turned and gave her a sheepish look. 'I'm sorry,' he said. 'I'm not being very good company.' Julie glanced behind her. Caroline was still engrossed in her music.

'She was only trying to show you what she could do. I think she wants you to be proud of her.'

'I know,' Pierre admitted. 'It was just, for a moment there, I thought the worst. She frightened me almost to death.'

'Then you should explain. She'll understand.'

'I know. And I will.' He drew his hand through his thick, dark hair. 'I never thought it would be so difficult to have responsibility for someone else. I'm used to responsibility, God knows, with work, the vineyards. But not for people. Except my patients, of course.' He looked at Julie and his face relaxed for the first time since Caroline had gone missing. 'But you, you are very good with people. It's what makes you a fine doctor.'

'Why, thank you, Dr Favatier,' Julie said lightly, but she couldn't help feeling pleased.

They drove on for a few minutes in silence. They were coming to the edge of the city. Half an hour at the most and they'd be home. Julie's thoughts drifted to the day they'd spent together. She had enjoyed herself, she realised. Pierre, except for the last incident, had been easy company. More than that, she admitted. Remembering the feel of his arms around her, the long length of his body under hers, when they'd had the snow fight, her spine tingled. She had wanted to stay there for ever. Hopeless though it was, she knew, for the first time since Luke had walked out of the hospital, leaving her alone, she was attracted to a man. Not just attracted, she admitted, but lust driven. But of all the people to develop a crush on! She cringed inwardly. Dr Pierre Favatier would never look twice at her. Besides, there was his girlfriend—Katherine. She felt the blood rush to her cheeks. How mortifying and what a cliché—to have a crush on your boss. Well, there was nothing for it, she would just have to make sure he never guessed. Thankfully, he wasn't going to be around for long. If she could manage to avoid him, apart from work, no one would ever know. Then, when he was gone, she would get over it.

'Julie.' His voice broke into her thoughts. Her blush deepened. Thank goodness the car was dark. 'I wonder if you would consider doing me a favour? I know I have no right to ask you—and you must feel free to say no.' Julie was curious.

'I have to go back to France in a few days. The manager of the vineyard needs me to sign some papers and sort some problems out.'

Julie's heart sank. She would miss seeing him around, even in the short time he was away. Was he going to ask her to keep an eye on Caroline? That would be okay, Julie thought. Caroline could always come and stay at her flat. It was small, but they would cope.

'Do you own the vineyards?'

'I own half, the other half belongs to Jacques—or Caroline now. My brother wanted to give me his share. Once he met Iona and moved to Scotland, he had no interest in the vineyard. I agreed to look after his half for him. Not that I can spare much time either, with my work. That is why I employ a manager.'

'Then what did Caroline mean when she said you had stolen her father's heritage?'

'She knew her father had given me his share, but not that I put it in a trust for her. She will inherit when she is twenty-one, or sooner if I think she's ready.'

'Does she know?'

'Jacques and I agreed that she shouldn't know until she was older. Of course he had no idea he wouldn't be around when she turned twenty-one.' He clenched his jaw and took a deep breath before continuing. 'The vineyard, and the money her grandfather left, is worth a considerable sum of money, and neither of us thought it would be a good thing for her to grow up believing she'd never have to worry about earning a living. Not that she'll ever have to, if she doesn't want to.'

'And this favour you want to ask me?'

He hesitated 'I want Caroline to come with me to France. I want her to begin to understand what it means to have responsibility. The vineyard employs many locals.'

'And don't you think she'll come with you? Do you want me to talk to her?' Julie couldn't help the pang of regret she felt at the way Pierre seemed to regard her as a means to an end. Then she berated herself. Of course he saw her that way. Why else would he seek out her company?

'No, I'll talk to her. She has a mid-term break coming up so time off school isn't a problem. But I think she'll try to insist that she stays here in Scotland while I am away.'

'If she won't go with you, she could come and stay with me, if that would help?'

Pierre glanced at her and smiled bleakly. 'You are a good friend to us, Julie.' Once again Julie felt her heart drop. Good friend—huh.

'But that's not what I want to ask you.' He continued. 'My hospital, the one I usually work at—I think you'd find it interesting to see.' He paused, as if searching for the right words. 'No, Julie, I want to ask you if you will come with us.'

'Me?' Julie spluttered. 'You want me to go with you? To France?'

'I know I have no right to ask you, but if you were to come, I think Caroline would come too. She likes you.'

But what about you? Julie fumed inwardly. How do you feel?

'If its female company you want for her, why don't you ask your girlfriend? Katherine—isn't that her name?'

'Katherine is no longer my girlfriend, as you put it. When I told her I'd be going skiing instead of taking her away for the weekend, she wasn't happy. She said I had to choose. So I did.' He shot Julie a small smile. 'It was never anything serious anyway.'

She couldn't help a hidden smile of delight at the thought that Pierre was no longer involved with a woman. Even though, no doubt, it was hardly likely to stay like that for long. But at least he was putting his niece's needs first for the time being.

'I don't know if I can get off work,' she prevaricated. But she knew she had tons of annual leave to take. It was just that her heart was pounding with excitement, making it difficult for her to breathe. A week in France with Pierre. Being with him, seeing him work, in his home environment. It was a fantastic opportunity. But what had she just been telling herself? That she needed to avoid him, for the sake of her pride if not her heart, and here she was contemplating spending a week in close proximity with him. Talk about heavenly torture.

'Of course. You have your own life. It was only a thought. Please, forget I asked.' He shrugged, but Julie could see he was disappointed.

It was only a few days. Surely she could keep her feelings under control for that length of time?

'Okay,' she found herself saying. 'If Caroline wants me to, that is.'

Pierre looked thrilled.

'*C'est le pied!* That's good. We leave next weekend.'

Over the next week, Julie could hardly believe that she had agreed to go to France with Pierre. He had told her when he

saw her at work on Monday that Caroline was delighted she
was going too, and had told him that no way would she go if
Julie hadn't agreed to.

Every time she was in his company she felt awkward and
tongue-tied. Except when they were seeing patients or operating. Only then did her feelings of self-consciousness disappear. To her chagrin, she found she was taking longer in the
mornings to get dressed, critically surveying her appearance
before, with an impatient sigh of regret, turning away from
the mirror and reaching for her usual workday clothes. But,
she had to admit, her cheeks had gained colour and her eyes
sparkled. She tried to tell herself that it was because she was
loving her job, the excitement of new challenges, of stretching herself as a doctor, but, in her more honest moments, she
knew she was kidding herself. It was thinking about him,
seeing him every day, that brought the sparkle to her eye and
a hippity-hop to her heart. She fancied him—she fancied him
like crazy.

When Kim heard Julie was to spend a few days in France
with Pierre, she was agog.

'You lucky old so-and-so,' she said. 'There will be more
than woman wanting to cut your heart out when they hear.'

They were in the duty room. Julie had just finished rounds
with Pierre, who had gone off to confer with his senior colleagues about a training issue, and Kim was, unusually for her,
taking a lunch-break. 'You didn't tell me anything over the
phone the other night. Go on, spill the beans. Did you…? I
mean, when you found yourselves alone in a romantic
hideaway—was that when…?'

Despite herself, Julie had to laugh. Her friend had being
trying to matchmake for her for years—with no success. Julie

had refused point blank to go on any of the dates her friend had tried to arrange.

'It wasn't like that at all,' Julie said firmly. 'As I've told you many times before, he sees me as a companion to his niece. I think he sees me as a lifeline. Maybe even as an excuse not to have to deal with Caroline at all.'

Her friend looked unconvinced. 'If you're right, and I am not saying you are at all, how do you feel about that? Don't you mind, well, being used?'

Julie felt a blush warm her cheeks. 'I don't feel as if I'm being used. Caroline reminds me so much of myself when I was her age. I like her.'

Kim eyed Julie suspiciously. 'You're blushing,' she said accusingly. 'My God, you do have a crush on him! Oh, Julie, don't get hurt.'

'A minute ago you were suggesting that we were having an affair, and now you are warning me off him.' Julie tried a laugh, but it was a strangled sound.

'Julie, it's all right to have an affair with men like Pierre. And I was only kidding. I didn't think he was your type. Men like Pierre, well, they are heart-breakers. They are only in for the short haul. But, Julie, if ever there was a woman who was in it for keeps, it's you.'

'And I'm not the sort of woman Pierre would want, let alone fall in love with,' she said bitterly 'Look, Kim, you're barking up the wrong tree. Anyway, a minute ago you were suggesting we had a thing going.'

'Yes, but that was before I knew you fancied him!'

'Kim—' Julie started, just as her pager beeped. Seconds later Kim's went off too. The two women glanced at their pagers.

'I'm wanted in A and E,' Kim said, getting to her feet.

'Me, too,' said Julie. 'Come on, let's see what's up.' As the two women hurried off to the department, a short walk away, Julie turned to her friend. 'Please don't tell anyone about me going away with Pierre and Caroline. You know what the gossip is like in this place.'

'Don't worry, kid, your secret is safe with me. Both of them.'

The accident and emergency department was a hive of activity. One of the staff nurses hurried over to Kim as soon as she saw her arrive.

'There's been an explosion in one of the chemical factories on the outskirts of the city. We've been put on major incident alert.'

'How many casualties and when are we expecting them to arrive?' Kim asked, all business.

'They can't tell us as yet. All we know is that there are at least five seriously hurt, possibly more. They say there are crush injuries as well as chemical burns...' She turned to Julie. 'That's why we called Plastics. Not everyone is accounted for yet.'

In the melee, Julie could see Pierre's tall frame above the heads of the nurses and doctors rushing about, making their preparations to receive the casualties. Leaving her friend to get on with her job, she went over to Pierre, who was talking to the department manager. He seemed unaware of her presence as she stood beside him.

'The patients will need to go through a disinfecting process,' he was saying. 'Make sure one is set up to the side of the department. You'll be clearing the department of all non-life-threatening injuries, I imagine?'

'It's being done as we speak,' said the manager, a tall woman in her early fifties Julie knew by sight if not by name.

'Unfortunately the constant threat of terrorist attacks in the UK means that we have plans for all sorts of emergencies, including ones like this so, Dr Favatier, you can relax. We know what we're doing.' The woman turned away to talk to another couple of doctors who had presented themselves at the department. Pierre looking pleased to see Julie, flashed her a smile.

'Good. They paged you.'

'What would you like me to do?' Julie's heart was beating rapidly, though whether as a reaction to the emergency or to Pierre's smile she couldn't be sure.

'When the casualties arrive, our job will be to work with the emergency doctors to ensure that any patients with chemical burns are treated appropriately. Obviously saving lives is the priority, but if we can ensure that their burns are treated properly right from the start, there will be less chance of patients needing corrective surgery later. *D'accord*?'

At Julie's nod, he went on to explain the course of action they would take as patients arrived. 'You must be careful you don't transfer any of the chemicals onto your own skin,' he warned, gripping her shoulder in a vice-like grip, his eyes boring into hers. 'No matter how—what is the word I'm looking for? Agitated?—things get, you must promise me you'll be careful.'

'I'll be careful,' Julie replied.

Outside they could hear the wail of ambulances. At least three, Julie thought, and there was bound to be more following.

'Stay close to me. If you are not sure, ask.' He lifted a hand as if he was about to touch her face, then just as quickly dropped it. 'Remember, stay safe.'

The next few hours passed in a blur for Julie as she fought to keep up with Pierre. Gone was the laconic attitude she had come to know. Instead, he worked with the single-minded concentration Julie saw in him when he operated. All the while he explained to Julie exactly what he was doing and why. Out of the seven serious casualties that were admitted, three had sustained major burns and required surgery.

It was after six by the time they finished operating. As the last patient was wheeled out of Theatre and into Recovery, Pierre straightened his shoulders. He had been bent over the operating table for the last three hours. His height in Theatre was a disadvantage, the table being set at a level appropriate for the majority of staff, Julie and the scrub nurse included. He looks tired, she thought, but then as she too stretched her aching muscles she realised he wasn't the only one.

Removing his mask and peeling off his gloves, Pierre looked at her sharply.

'Are you okay?' he asked, frowning.

'I'm fine,' Julie replied a little more abruptly than she'd intended. 'Nothing a sandwich and a cup of coffee won't put right, at any rate.'

'Thank you, everyone,' Pierre said to the rest of the exhausted team. 'Well done.' There were smiles and nods of appreciation as the theatre team set about tidying up the theatre in preparation for the morning. Pierre turned to Julie.

'You should go home and get some rest,' he said. 'We have another busy day tomorrow.'

'I'm fine,' Julie said. 'In fact, I feel so full of adrenaline I doubt I could sleep anyway.' As they were talking, they were walking towards the changing room. Pierre glanced at Julie. 'I know exactly what you mean,' he said. 'I feel the same way after I operate. After surgery I often go on my motorbike for a drive into the country. Afterwards I usually sleep like an infant.'

'A baby,' Julie corrected automatically. Then she noticed Pierre's look of puzzlement. 'Sleep like a baby. That's the expression in English.'

'*D'accord*. Sleep like a baby,' he grinned. 'Would you like to come too?'

'What? For a spin? On your bike?' She thought for a moment, imagining herself flying along at speed, the wind in her face, her arms wrapped around Pierre. Damn it! Why were her thoughts always going in the wrong direction as far as he was concerned?

'You'll be safe with me, I promise. And after, we will have something to eat. *Non*?' He looked at Julie a twinkle in his eyes.

He makes me feel five years old, she mused. As if I'm a child to whom he's offering a trip to the fairground. But then she made up her mind. What the hell! Why do I have to be so bloody cautious all the time? Why can't I just let myself have fun for once? Live for the moment and to hell with the consequences!

'Why not?' she said.

CHAPTER SIX

By the time Julie emerged from surgical block, Pierre was waiting for her, casually leaning against a wall while demolishing an apple with evident enjoyment. He had changed into jeans and a T-shirt with only a leather jacket for warmth. Julie's heart gave a traitorous leap. Why did he have to be so damn good-looking and so self-assured? And why did she feel so dowdy and uninteresting next to him? For once she wished she was the glamorous type.

Even to Julie's untrained eye his bike, all gleaming metal and chrome, looked as if it was built for speed. The night was dark and cloudless, cold with the sharpness of frost in the air. Julie wondered if it was going to snow again. She shivered. Hopefully in the South of France it would be warmer. Although she was used to the cold, a little warmth in the middle of winter would be welcome.

'I'm sorry to have kept you waiting,' she said. 'And you're going to have to wait even longer while I shower and change. There's no way I can eat without freshening up.'

'*De rien*,' he replied. 'The apple will keep the animals from the door.'

'Wolf from the door,' Julie responded automatically.

'Animals, wolves—whatever. My English expressions get mixed up sometimes.' Removing a helmet tied onto the seat, he handed it to her. 'I have learned always to have a spare one,' he said.

I bet you have, Julie thought glumly. *I bet you are always prepared for company. Especially the feminine kind.*

Taking hold of the helmet, she pulled it on over her head and hopped up behind Pierre. Self-conscious at the sudden intimacy, she shrank away from him, letting her hands hang by her sides. Pierre reached behind him and pulled her arms around his waist. Accepting she had no choice, she slipped her hands under his jacket, acutely conscious of the feel of hard muscle under her fingertips.

'Where to first?' he asked.

'Why don't we go up Arthur's Seat?' she suggested. 'It's not far and you get great views of the city from there.'

'Okay. But you need to hold on,' he said. Julie was glad that the helmet hid the tell-tale blush that she could feel creeping into her cheeks. She really should have outgrown the childish habit by now, she thought, exasperated with herself.

He revved up the powerful machine and with a squeal of tyres pulled away. The impetus of the bike forced Julie to hold on tighter. For a moment she was tempted to lean her head against his back but, thank God, prevented herself just in time. It was one thing to have her arms wrapped around him, quite another to be cuddling into his back!

They sped through the early evening traffic. As she held on, Julie gave herself up to the moment. For a short while she let herself imagine that she was being driven away into the unknown with a man who wanted nothing more than to steal her away, and keep her all to himself. Somewhere isolated and romantic—the South of France would do for a start. The image was so startling she almost let go of Pierre. Now, where did that come from? she wondered. She had never been the type of woman to indulge in romantic daydreams. Was it because Pierre was French, exotic? Whatever the reason, that way of thinking had no place in her well-ordered, if boring life.

He turned up the road leading to the top of the hill. They sped to the top before Pierre pulled over at the highest point. They both climbed off the bike. Below them the lights of Edinburgh sparkled as far as the eye could see.

'It is a beautiful city,' Pierre said. 'Almost as beautiful as Paris.'

'I love it,' Julie said. 'Although it does get crowded in the summer with all the visitors.'

'Have you ever visited my city?' Pierre asked.

'Once, when I was younger. But I thought your home was in the South of France.'

'I work in Paris. That's where the hospital is. I go south whenever I have time off. Which isn't a lot.'

Up on the top of the hill the air was freezing. Julie shivered, pulling her jacket tighter.

'I am sorry. You are cold,' Pierre said, removing his jacket and wrapping it around Julie's shoulders.

She snuggled into the leather, breathing in the now familiar smell of his scent.

'That's the castle over there,' she said, pointing to her left, 'and to the right is Scott's monument. Have you visited them?'

'I haven't had time yet. One day, perhaps.'

They stood in silence for a few moments.

'I thought you would have been here many times—to see

your family,' Julie said. Caroline had mentioned that he'd never been to visit, but perhaps in her anger she'd exaggerated?

She felt Pierre move way from her.

'I should have come,' he said tightly. 'Of course I know that now. Had I known what was going to happen…'

'Why didn't you, then?'

He shrugged. 'I left for America to train before Jacques and Iona's wedding. I was there for five years. Somehow I never found the time to come to Scotland to see them.' Something in his voice made Julie wonder if he was telling the whole truth. Was he really suggesting that in five years he couldn't find a couple of weeks to visit his brother?

'You weren't close to Jacques, then?' she said. 'I guess not all families are.'

'I loved Jacques,' Pierre responded fiercely. 'There was no man I was prouder to call my brother. All our lives we were together, until he got married.'

'Was it her, then? Iona? Did you not get on with her?' Julie persisted. She didn't know why she felt the need to go on with the conversation, but she sensed that the key to understanding Pierre lay in knowing about his family.

Pierre laughed shortly. 'Iona! There is no one in this earth who wouldn't want to spend at least some of their life in her company.' He stopped abruptly. 'I did see them in France, once, before that last trip. At my father's funeral. They brought Caroline with them. She was about five years old. It was the first and last time I saw her until after the accident. She didn't even remember me! I wanted her to come and live with me in France. But how could I ask that of her? She had lost everything, I couldn't ask her to leave her home as well.'

'So you came here to be with her? That was good of you.'

'Good of me? Pah! I should have come sooner. It is too late now for me to make up for all the lost years,' he said bitterly.

Julie had never seen this side of him before. Her heart ached for him. She would have given anything to have been able to put her arms around him and comfort him. But of course that wasn't possible. She could imagine Pierre's shock if she did.

'Well, you're here now, with her. That's what matters,' she said softly.

Changing the subject, Pierre pointed out a shooting star. Julie watched entranced as they followed its descent.

'I would like to show you Paris,' he said eventually. 'The Eiffel Tower, Notre Dame, the Seine. I have seen it before, many times of course, but I would like to see it through someone else's—your—eyes.'

Julie felt a warmth suffuse her body. Was there a chance he was beginning to see her as a woman? Not just a colleague and a friend to his niece?

'But now,' he said, and laughed, breaking the moment, 'I am hungry. Shall we go and eat?'

A short time later they drew up outside Julie's flat. She almost leapt off the bike in her haste to put some physical distance between them. She needed to keep him at arm's length to stop these unsettling, embarrassing fantasies.

'Would you like to come up and wait?' she asked, thinking that she would much prefer him not to be in her flat.

'*Mais oui,*' Pierre replied, looking puzzled. 'I had not thought I would stay outside in the cold while you got changed. If you are like every other woman I know, that could mean a very long time.'

'It won't take me long to shower and change,' Julie replied, cringing. He must think her a bit of an idiot. 'Of course you should come up and wait.'

She opened the door, frantically thinking back to when she had left that morning. Had she tidied up? Put away the break-fast things? Picked up her clothes from the floor? House-keeping wasn't her strong point. She dashed inside, leaving Pierre to follow in her wake. Spotting a pair of discarded panties and T-shirt that she had slept in the night before, she quickly scooped them up and stuffed them under a cushion, hoping that Pierre didn't notice.

Pierre remained standing just inside the doorway.

'Please come in,' Julie said flustered. 'Make yourself at home.'

Pierre removed a pile of textbooks from a chair and sat down, just as Toto stalked into the room. The cat made a beeline for Pierre and jumped into his lap. 'I think he remem-bers you,' she said reaching over to remove the cat from Pierre's lap.

'Hey, it's okay,' Pierre said, stroking Toto, who had already settled himself down as if it had become his favourite spot. 'I don't mind.'

'I found him outside a few months ago,' Julie said. 'The poor thing was half-starved. I took him to the animal shelter but they said they might have to put him down if no one claimed him. He's quite old, you see, and set in his ways. I thought it was unlikely he would find a new home, so I took him. I couldn't risk it.' Now what was she doing? Babbling on about her cat. She couldn't imagine Pierre finding anything less interesting.

But to her surprise he nodded, as if he understood what she

was saying. 'The farm I grew up on always had plenty of animals.' He said. 'Dogs, cats, horses, chickens. My mother was always rescuing animals. I have no space in my Paris flat otherwise I would probably have two or three animals of my own.'

It was a different side to Pierre. Up until now Julie had only thought of him as being a sophisticated man of the world. It hadn't occurred to her he had been brought up in the country, although if his father had owned a vineyard it was obvious really. The image of a small boy in short trousers running about the French countryside followed by a menagerie of animals flashed into her mind. The thought made her smile. Somehow she couldn't see it. It was too far removed from the way the way he appeared now.

'What is so funny?' Pierre asked.

'Nothing,' Julie said. 'I just hadn't thought of you as being brought up in the country.'

'But, then, you don't really know much about me, do you?' He raised an eyebrow. 'And I don't know very much about you either.' He smiled lazily. 'But I intend to find out more over dinner—if we ever get there,' he said, glancing at his watch.

Julie's heart missed a beat. Was he flirting with her?

'I'll be as quick as I can,' she said, bolting for the bathroom.

As she showered, she thought back to Pierre's words. He wanted to find out more about her. Well, why not? the sensible side of her answered. His niece has formed an attachment to you—of course he is going to want to find out all he can about you. It doesn't mean any more than that. So don't get your hopes up. Finishing her shower, she stood in front of the mirror and surveyed herself critically. She supposed her figure wasn't bad, although she couldn't say she liked her small breasts all that much. Maybe she could ask Pierre to give her a breast augmentation. She rolled her eyes at her reflection. No, actually, she was happy with the size they were. If only she could say the same about her face. When she smiled, it exaggerated the scar. Perhaps that was why she felt embarrassed when she smiled. Looking at her face made her spirits drop. Who was she kidding? Pierre flirting with *her*? This mousy, unattractive woman? But perhaps he really didn't notice her disfigurement? Maybe, being a plastic surgeon, he was more able to see behind superficial imperfection? Maybe he saw the real her. The one she had kept hidden for so long. The one, as Lexy had pointed out, who had so much to give.

She slipped into jeans and a roll-neck sweater, and blasted her hair briefly with a hairdryer. Finally she dabbed on a touch of foundation before adding a slick of lipstick and thickening her lashes with mascara. Fastening her watch back onto her wrist, she noticed that it had taken her just over fifteen minutes to shower and change. Not bad, she thought with some satisfaction. She'd told Pierre she wouldn't be long.

By the time she returned to the sitting room Pierre was leaning back in the chair with his eyes closed. If it were not for the fact he was absent-mindedly stroking Toto, who had turned over on his back and seemed ecstatic with the attention he was receiving, Julie would have thought Pierre was asleep. Like most surgeons, he seemed to have the knack of finding a few moments to rest whenever he could. Once again the thought of those long fingers stroking her skin flashed through her mind. She could almost feel them touching her back, caressing her neck. What would it be like to be loved by this man? She shook her head impatiently. What was the use of thinking like that? She would never know. All of a sudden Pierre's eyes flickered open. He looked at her through alf-closed eyes. For a moment, as he stared deep into her yes, she thought she saw a flicker of desire.

Just as quickly as the thought entered her head, she knew he was mistaken. Pierre uncoiled himself from the chair and tretched, his T-shirt riding above his jeans, and Julie caught a glimpse of bronzed lean muscle.

'Ready? *Alors. Allons-y*,' he said.

Julie suggested to Pierre that they walk to her favourite talian restaurant, a short distance from her flat. She ate there often after work when she was too tired to cook or had simply not got around to shopping for food. The manageress, a flamboyant curly-headed Italian called Isobella, knew her well, and as soon as she noticed Julie's arrival she came up to greet her, depositing two wet kisses on each of Julie's cheeks.

'My favourite doctor,' she said in a voice that echoed around the dining room, much to Julie's embarrassment. She had entirely forgotten about Isobella and her complete disregard for British rectitude. 'I haven't seen you for a long time. Where have you been hiding?' Then, before Julie had a chance to reply, she turned her attention to Pierre. 'And who is this? Your young man? Good. It is about time you brought someone in to meet us.'

For the umpteenth time Julie felt herself cringe in Pierre's company. Now he would think she was trying to pass him off as her boyfriend or, at the very least, realise that she was never in the company of a man. But Pierre seemed unfazed by Isobella. Instead, he took her hand and pressed it to his lips. On anyone else the gesture would have seemed theatrical, almost effeminate, but from Pierre it just seemed perfectly natural. Pierre spoke to the proprietor in rapid Italian. Julie had no idea what he said, but it was enough to make the older woman blush and smile coyly. 'Ah, I think you are a lucky woman,' she said to Julie as she showed them to their table.

'I didn't realise you spoke Italian too! What did you say to her?' Julie asked, taking her seat as Isobella hurried away to find them some menus.

'I told her it was me who was lucky to have you as a dinner companion. And, yes, I speak Italian. Most of my countrymen do.'

'You said a damn sight more than that,' Julie retorted, but Pierre just smiled. 'Ah, well. You'll just have to learn to speak Italian and French if you truly want to know what is being said,' Pierre responded.

'Touché. It is a bit of a disgrace I can't manage more than a little French and a smattering of Spanish. I keep promising I'll go to evening classes to learn, but there never seem to be enough hours in the day.'

When Isobella returned with the menus, they ordered their meals. Julie chose Carbonara and Pierre decided on a pizza. 'In fact, make that two,' he called out as their waiter was leaving.

'I don't want pizza as well as pasta,' Julie protested.

'Good,' Pierre replied. 'Because they are both for me.' Remembering the feel of the hard muscle of his chest and abdomen under her fingers when they had been on the bike, Julie marvelled at his appetite. But Pierre wolfed down his meal as if the food was just an appetiser. As they ate they chatted. Pierre ordered a bottle of wine and as she sipped her first glass, she felt herself relax. He was an amusing and charming dinner companion. He told her about his upbringing on the farm where his family had been growing grapes for generations.

'I look forward to showing it to you,' he told Julie.

'And I look forward to seeing it,' she replied, taking another sip of her wine. The warmth of the alcohol was spreading through her body. She rarely drank, but the wine was dissipating the discomfort she felt in Pierre's presence. My goodness, she thought, is it getting warm in here?

'Now tell me about you,' he said, looking interested. 'What was growing up like for you?'

'I've always lived in Edinburgh—when I wasn't away, skiing,' Julie said. 'I started going away with the club when I was about eight years old.'

Pierre looked at her, his eyes holding her gaze.

'That must have been hard for a young girl. To be away from her family.'

'I suppose I got used to it.' Julie said lightly. But she was recalling, only too vividly, the awful feelings of homesickness she had suffered from almost as soon as her parents had waved her off. The adults who had travelled with them had tried to be supportive, but it hadn't been the same as having your own family around. For the first time Julie wondered whether it was part of the reason she had never really felt as if she belonged anywhere.

Encouraged by Pierre, she told him about her parents, the fact she was an only child, how shocked and desperately worried they had been when she'd had her accident and finally how understanding they had been throughout everything.

'I guess I was angry with the world for a while,' she admitted. 'For so many years I had thought of nothing else but skiing. I had set my sights on the Olympics and really believed I had a chance.'

'But after you recovered?' Pierre probed gently, 'Couldn't you have gone back? Made a comeback?'

'I had missed too much training time. Every week counts at that level, and I was out for almost four months. Then my boyfriend—Luke—left me.' She stared into her wineglass.

Pierre must have seen something of the anguish of those few months in her eyes. He stretched a hand across the table and grasped her fingers in his.

'Pauvre petite,' he said. 'You had a bad time.'

Julie felt her hand tremble under his. 'The worst thing was, when I first got out of hospital, I went a bit mad. I neglected my studies. I wouldn't go anywhere or see anyone, or even come out of my room. I must have driven Mum and Dad mad with worry.' She took another sip of wine. She was beginning to feel pleasantly sleepy.

'My parents eventually made me realise that I needed to set my sights somewhere—that I needed something else to strive for. They suggested medicine, and the minute I thought about it I knew they were right. During the months I spent in hospital I drove the nurses and doctors crazy. First of all with my questions about my injuries, then I started following them about, demanding to know what was wrong with everyone else. Eventually, to shut me up they brought me medical journals and textbooks and told me to find out myself.' She paused once again, suddenly realising that she must be boring Pierre.

'I'm sorry,' she said, horrified. 'I don't usually go on about myself in this way!'

'No, please.' Pierre said his eyes warm. 'I want to know. Tell me about your parents. Caroline told me they are no longer living.'

Julie repeated what she had told Caroline, although this time she tried to make light of how excluded from the family circle she had always felt. She didn't want him feeling sorry for her.

But it seemed as if Pierre wasn't deceived. 'It must have been hard for you,' he said softly.

'It wasn't as if they didn't love me,' Julie said. 'And besides I have always had my work and my friends. I have had—have—a good life,' she insisted fiercely. 'My parents sacrificed a lot for me. They weren't well off, you know. Sending me abroad took almost every penny they earned.'

'They must have been proud of you,' Pierre said. He reached for her hand and stroked it almost absent-mindedly. Julie felt a river of desire ripple through her body. She removed her hand from his.

'They were. Not always—but at the end. Yes. I think they were.' Mortified, she was aware her eyes had moistened. Impatiently she blinked the tears away. She didn't want Pierre to see them. He looked at her, his blue eyes the colour of a winter sky, and she returned his look defiantly. 'I only told Caroline so she would know that I understand what she's going through.'

'Ah. The tough Dr McKenzie, who works and skis harder and better than any man. Who doesn't need anything or anyone.' He looked at her with narrowed eyes. 'I wonder.'

Julie thought it was time to change the subject. She was beginning to feel something electric in the air between them. She didn't know what it was, but it was making her feel giddy. 'Would you like pudding?' she asked.

Pierre ordered biscuits and cheese but Julie, full after her rich pasta dish, declined. As he made short work of it he insisted she tell him more, seeming genuinely interested.

'There's not much more to tell,' Julie said. 'Instead of going out all the time, I hid myself in my room and began to study like mad to get the grades I needed to go to medical school. I had neglected my studies for so long, it took some catching up.'

'Lucky you are clever.' Pierre nodded.

'I suppose,' Julie admitted reluctantly. 'But I think it was also the determination to make something out of my life.' She looked at him from under her lashes. 'The rest, as they say, is history. Medical school followed by the usual rotations, and now here I am in Surgery.'

'You will be an excellent surgeon, I have no doubt. But what do you do when you're not working?'

Julie felt herself open up under his interested gaze. It seemed he really did want to know. 'I ski, I read and I visit St Margaret's Hospice. After my mother died, I carried on visiting. If you want to see real courage, you don't have to look much further than the patients, and their families who depend on it. Getting to know some of them has been a real lesson for me.'

'In what way?'

'They made me realise that I had been blessed to have had the opportunities I did. That if all I had to worry about was my face, I was lucky.'

Pierre lifted his hand and, stretching across the table, trailed a long finger down her scar.

'I have seen much worse than this,' he said. 'You are still a very attractive woman.'

Julie felt a shiver run through her body. He's only being kind, she told herself. Wasn't he?

'Luke obviously didn't think so,' she said, trying to keep the bitterness from her voice.

'Then he is a fool,' Pierre said harshly.

Could Pierre mean what he was saying? Did he really think

she was attractive? Could he see past the scar to the woman underneath? Did he suspect how much she needed to believe that one day she would find someone to love her? She knew she had so much love to give.

'What about you?' she ventured, emboldened by the wine. 'Have you ever been in love?'

Immediately the shutters came down. His eyes looked bleak and his mouth twisted. He sat back in his chair, crossing his arms across his chest. 'Once,' he said shortly. Something in his expression warned Julie not to probe further, and if to make it clear that the subject was off limits, Pierre called for the bill.

'We'd better get you home,' he said. 'Remember we are leaving for France tomorrow. Our plane is at twelve. I have your ticket. I can give it to you at the airport.'

They collected their coats, with Isobella fussing around them. 'Good girl,' she whispered in Julie's ear. 'You have a handsome one there.'

There wasn't an opportunity for Julie to set the record straight. Besides, she was finding that it took all her concentration for her to stop the restaurant whirling about as if she was on a merry-go-round. She didn't think she had drunk very much, but, then again, she had only been vaguely aware of the waiter at her elbow, refilling her glass.

Outside the restaurant she held out her hand to Pierre. 'Goodnight,' she hiccuped. 'Oops!' she said, covering her mouth with her hand.

Pierre looked amused. 'I left my motorbike at your flat,' he reminded her. 'Even if I hadn't, I still think it's a good idea that I walk you home. I don't want you breaking an ankle before tomorrow.'

'Actually, that would be very kind of you, Pierre.' Julie

could manage the words, it was just that her legs didn't seem to want to obey her. Julie knew it was Pierre's closeness rather than the alcohol that was making her feel unsteady.

'I should come in to make sure you're okay,' Pierre said when they arrived outside Julie's flat.

'I'm fine!' she insisted, but noticing the determined set of his jaw realised that it would be futile to argue with him.

When they got inside, Julie turned to thank Pierre. He must have been closer than she had realised because as she turned she bumped against him. For a moment the world disappeared as she found herself staring into his expressive blue eyes. Before she knew how it had happened, his arms were around her and he was kissing her hungrily. She let herself melt into him, feeling the hard length of his body. He moved his lips to her neck. She arched, letting her head fall back, giving herself up to the sensations which were pulsing through her body. She felt as if she was drowning as wave upon wave of desire hit her. Suddenly, without warning, he pulled away from her. He looked down at her, breathing deeply. Julie was conscious of her own breaths coming in shallow gasps.

'Please, forgive me,' he said, and moved away from her towards the door. 'I had no right. It was unforgivable.'

Julie was bewildered. A moment ago he had been kissing her as if he would never stop. Now he was looking at her as if…almost as if he disliked her. Had it been her that had turned into his arms? Did he think she had thrown herself at him? Poor lonely disfigured Julie, trying to seduce the handsome rich Pierre. She was mortified. How had it happened?

'I'm…I'm sorry,' Julie said, cringing. She tried to laugh it off. 'I must have had too much wine at dinner. I don't usually get into clinches with my boss.'

'It is I who has to apologise,' he said stiffly. 'Not you.' He looked as if he didn't know what to do next. 'It was me who kissed you. I shouldn't have done that. We work together—it was unprofessional.'

Julie wasn't sure she believed his explanation. Pierre didn't strike her as the type of man who let anything get in the way of what he wanted. He was probably just being kind. Trying to remove himself from an embarrassing situation as gently as possible. No doubt he had plenty of practice in fielding besotted women.

She tried a smile, hoping he wouldn't see the effort it caused her. 'It was just a kiss, nothing serious,' she said. 'Let's forget it ever happened.' But it hadn't been just a kiss. She could have sworn there had been more in the way he'd kissed her. But, then again, as she knew only too well, she didn't have much experience of men. So who was she to judge?

He stayed by the door, looking as if he wanted to say something else.

'I think you should go, don't you?' Julie said, desperate to hang onto the last shreds of her dignity.

He shook his head as if angry with himself. '*D'accord*,' he said. 'I will see you tomorrow.' And then, with a click of the door, he was gone.

CHAPTER SEVEN

JULIE awoke the next morning to a throbbing headache. She had tossed and turned all night, unable to stop thinking about what had happened. The more she thought about it, the more she convinced herself she had instigated the kiss. And if he had responded, well wasn't that the reaction of any normal red-blooded male? She groaned, hiding herself underneath the blanket. She could just stay there and never come out, she thought. Never face Pierre again. She felt her cheeks burn. Then she remembered. God! She was going to France with him—if he still wanted her to go, that was. But why would he? The man would obviously want to keep his distance from his sex-starved junior. She groaned again. He was her boss! How could she, even for one second, have forgotten?

The phone rang. Julie eyed it blearily. Maybe if she ignored it, whoever it was would go away. But it kept on ringing. Reluctantly, Julie picked up the receiver.

'Hello,' she croaked.

'Hey, Julie, Uncle Pierre asked me to call you to make sure you were up.' It was Caroline. Had Pierre said anything to his niece about the night before? Somehow Julie knew he wouldn't have. Despite his easy Gallic charm, Pierre was too much of a gentleman to gossip about women. Even those who tried to kiss them. Julie groaned again.

'What's that?' Caroline asked anxiously. 'The line isn't very good. Are you feeling all right? Pierre said you might have eaten something that didn't agree with you last night. Oh! Please say you are still going to come.'

'I don't know,' Julie mumbled. 'I really don't feel all that well. I've an awful headache.' Well it was true, her head did ache. So did her heart, for that matter. Out of the two she would chose the headache any day.

'You must come,' Caroline said fiercely. 'You must. Otherwise I shan't go either. You know I wouldn't have agreed to go in the first place if you hadn't said you'd come too. Please, Julie.'

Julie could hear the desperation in Caroline's voice. She wondered why the girl was so reluctant to go without her. But she had promised—and she didn't break promises.

'What time is it?' she asked, squinting at her wristwatch.

'Eight-thirty. We have to check in in an hour.'

Julie managed to focus on the hands of her watch. It couldn't be eight-thirty already. But it was! And she hadn't even packed. She threw aside the bedclothes and headed for the shower.

'I'll meet you at the airport,' she said to Caroline.

'Uncle Pierre told me to let you know we'd collect you,' Caroline replied. But the last person Julie wanted to see right now was Pierre. Sure, she'd have to face him sooner or later, but the longer she could put off the inevitable the better.

'Airport—nine-thirty or nothing,' she said firmly.

'Okay,' Caroline said, and Julie could hear the relief in her voice. 'Anything you say. I'll tell Pierre. See you soon.' And with that she disconnected the call.

Julie hadn't time to think as she showered, before throwing her clothes into a suitcase. The hot, cascading water had revived her a bit, but she found she couldn't face breakfast. The thought of facing Pierre was making her head spin. What should she do? Pretend it had never happened? Apologise? What on earth would he be thinking? She cringed. What else would he think except that she was some hero-worshiping woman who was desperate to get him into her bed? Well, there was no point in imagining what he was thinking. She would just have to wait and take her lead from him. Hopefully she could persuade him that her actions had all been down to the wine she'd drunk at dinner. That was better than him suspecting, even for a moment, that she fancied him rotten!

Caroline was waiting for her outside Departures when she arrived at the airport. Noticing the look of relief when she saw Julie coming towards her, Julie was glad that she had put her own feelings aside and come.

'You made it!' Caroline said, before reverting to her usual casual attitude. 'Cool.' She took Julie's bag and marched off. 'Uncle Pierre is waiting for us in the business lounge. We'll just get you checked in, then we can meet him.'

All too soon, Julie was checked in and inside the business lounge. Pierre stood to meet them, a coffee-cup in his hand.

'*Bonjour*,' he said. 'Did you sleep well?'

'Yes. Thank you,' Julie mumbled

'And are you feeling better? Caroline said you had a headache.' He looked at her over the top of Caroline's head, but Julie couldn't read his expression. 'Coffee?' he suggested. This time there was no mistaking the glint of humour in his dark eyes. 'Caroline, would you mind fetching Julie a *café au lait*?'

They watched as Caroline helped herself from the table.

'About last night,' Julie muttered. 'Can we forget it ever happened?' She had to say something.

'*D'accord*. It is forgotten.'

'Naturally, it won't happen again,' Julie added.

'*C'est dommage*,' Pierre said so quietly that Julie couldn't be sure she had heard him correctly. Had he said it was a shame? She glanced at him, but then Caroline returned with a tray of coffee and biscuits.

'They say we are to board in five minutes,' she said. 'So we'd better hurry.'

Once they had finished their drinks they boarded their aircraft. Julie was seated next to Caroline with Pierre in the seat in front next to the exit. Typically he had managed to charm the ground staff into allocating him a seat with extra room to accommodate his long legs. As the plane taxied for take-off, Caroline slid her hand into Julie's. She looked at her young companion, to find her almost rigid with terror.

'Are you frightened of flying?' Julie whispered.

'I wasn't,' Caroline said through clenched teeth. 'But it's the first time I've flown since Mama and Papa…' She tailed off and Julie could see a tear slip out from her tightly clenched eyes. How could she have forgotten? Of course the girl was bound to be nervous—her parents had only recently been killed in a plane crash. Apart from that there were the memories of going back to the last place her parents had been before they'd died. She gripped Caroline's hand more tightly.

'Just breathe deeply,' she said. 'In and out—slowly— through your nose. That's what I used to do before a race. It always worked for me.'

By the time the seat-belt lights were switched off, some

colour had returned to her companion's cheeks. I need to remember why I am here, Julie reminded herself. It has nothing to do with Pierre and everything to do with this grief-stricken girl next to me. She could only guess how much courage it had taken Caroline to agree to this trip.

'Tell me about France. When were you last there?' she said, as much to distract the girl as from her own intense curiosity about Pierre's home.

'I haven't been there since I was about five. We used to go every summer to see Grandpère, but once he died we stopped going. I'm not sure why.'

'What's it like?'

'The house is on the northern edge of the vineyards. It's old-fashioned. Like a farmhouse. I love it.'

'Who lives there now?' Julie asked. 'As I understand it, Pierre lives in Paris.'

'The manager of the vineyard and his family stay there at the moment,' she replied.

'Have you ever thought about moving back?' Julie asked.

'I don't know. I don't know where home is any more! Maybe I can leave things the way they are indefinitely.' Once again there was that hesitation. 'Pierre thinks one day I might like to come back to France to live.'

'Why did your parents not live in France?' Julie asked. 'Your grandfather must have hoped at least one of his sons would take on the running of the vineyard?'

Caroline turned her head away and looked out of the window for a few moments, as if considering her reply.

'They did. Live in France. At least, until I was born. Then we moved back to Scotland. Papa always said it was because Mama wanted to live in her homeland. But I don't know.

Whenever she spoke about France, she always seemed so sad. As if she missed it very much.'

'I guess you can love a country but not want to live there,' Julie volunteered.

'I suppose. But my father really missed his home. I know that. And my mother would have done anything for his happiness. It never did make sense to me,' she said wistfully. 'And now I'll never know how they really felt. I always thought there was so much time to talk to them, to get to know them as adults and not just as my parents.' Her voice broke and Julie's heart went out to her.

'At least you are going to see the place they loved again,' she said sympathetically.

'The last place they were before they died. I wish I had gone with them. If it wasn't for my stupid exams I would have been with them,' the girl said miserably.

'And you would have died, too,' Julie reminded her softly.

'I wouldn't have minded,' Caroline said, the tears now flowing in earnest. 'Anything would be better than this. I miss them so much!'

Julie undid her seat belt and pulled the distraught girl into her arms, comforting her with soothing noises as she sobbed. Julie knew there wasn't much that she could say to comfort her. Grief like hers would just have to take its course. She wondered if Pierre really understood the depths of his niece's sorrow. Perhaps he was too wrapped up in his own life to notice? But, then again, he was bound to be suffering too. She had seen it in his eyes as he had looked at the photograph of his dead brother and sister-in-law. No, there was no mistaking he too felt their deaths deeply.

By the time they landed Caroline had regained her composure. They still had a long journey ahead, but Pierre wanted to stop at his Parisian flat to check for mail before they continued towards the South. If he noticed Caroline's swollen eyes as they collected their bags, he said nothing.

'You two can carry on without me, if you want,' he suggested. 'I can catch the evening train, while you get the earlier one.'

'I want to see where you live,' Caroline said, surprising Julie. She had thought she had very little interest in her uncle's life. Pierre looked uncertain, and for a moment Julie wondered if he had arranged to meet someone at his flat. A girlfriend perhaps?

'*D'accord*,' he said, smiling. 'As you wish.'

Pierre's apartment was near the centre of Paris—a beautiful Edwardian building with windows that stretched from the floor to ceiling. Inside it was exquisitely furnished and Julie wondered if Iona had had a hand in the interior design. It would have been natural for him to ask his sister-in-law, an artist and interior designer, to help furnish his place. Looking around at the oversized reception rooms with their graceful French antiques, Julie was beginning to really appreciate how wealthy Pierre actually was. The property, situated where it was, must be worth a fortune. But somehow, despite its beautiful furnishings, the flat seemed empty, devoid of a heart. Perhaps it was because Pierre had been away for a few weeks, but Julie didn't think so. It seemed to her that Pierre's home was no more than a place he ate and slept. Or perhaps took his women to, she thought, trying to ignore the way her spirits sank at the thought.

'This is wicked,' Caroline said approvingly. 'Maybe I can bring a few of my friends for a visit some time. I always wanted to see Paris.'

'We could spend a night here on our way back from the farm,' Pierre suggested. 'I could show you all the places I told you about. It's been years since I visited them myself,' he added ruefully. 'Somehow I never seem to find the time.'

Julie laughed. 'I think it's the same whatever city one lives in. I can't remember the last time I visited Edinburgh Castle or climbed the steps to Scott's monument.'

'Me neither,' agreed Caroline. 'But we should take Pierre when we get back—if he can spare the time.' She slid a look in her uncle's direction.

'We'll see,' he said. And then, catching Julie's warning look, added, 'But, yes, I would like that.'

It was late by the time they arrived at the vineyard and almost completely dark. Julie only had the vaguest notion of row upon row of bare-looking vines as they drove up to the main house. They had been collected from the station by a friendly-looking man in his late thirties. Pierre had introduced him as Alain—his friend and the manager of the vineyard.

The farmhouse was a large two-storey affair, and as Alain and Pierre carried the bags into the spacious hall, Julie immediately felt at home. The bedroom that was to be hers was on the first floor and furnished with a kingsize bed, made up with patchwork quilts and piles of pillows. A fire had been lit in the grate at one end of the room and its cheery glow cast its flickering light across the room.

After a quick wash she joined the others in the sitting room. Another fire had been lit there, this time in a fireplace which was at least twice the size of the one in her bedroom, which was just as well as the sitting room was bigger than any Julie had ever been in before. Large oversized sofas were positioned close to the fire, and Julie sank gratefully into the welcoming comfort of the one closest to the roaring flames.

I could live here for the rest of my life, Julie thought. It's just so perfect.

Michelle, Alain's wife, had flung her arms around Pierre when they had first arrived, clearly delighted to see him again. She had also fussed over Caroline. 'You look so much like your mama and papa, *ma petite*,' she had said sadly, before enfolding the girl in a hug. 'It is good to see you back where you belong.'

Julie was barely able to stay awake during dinner, a simple affair of bread, cheese and salad, and as soon as she politely could she excused herself, pleading tiredness, and sought the sanctuary of her bedroom. As she snuggled into bed, listening to the laughter coming from the kitchen, she felt inexplicably depressed. The atmosphere of the house, the warmth of the greeting, the laughter from below somehow made her feel more alone than ever. How she would love to be a part of loving family—to feel as if she really belonged, to feel as she was really loved. For years now she had thought that her career and Kim and Lexy was enough. That she wouldn't miss never having a partner and children of her own. But suddenly, devastatingly, she realised that was no longer true. Right now, she could imagine nothing she wanted more than to be a part of Pierre's life.

Julie woke to the sounds of birds singing and French voices calling to each other. Looking at her watch, she was horrified to find it was almost ten. She never slept that late! She sprang out of bed, and after a five-minute shower pulled on jeans and a blouse. Tying her hair into a plait, she coated her lips with a quick slick of gloss. Then for a moment she stood, arrested, in front of the mirror. For the first time since the accident she hadn't thought about hiding her scar. With her hair tied back and her face almost entirely devoid of make-up her scar was there for everyone to see. She peered in the mirror. Was it getting fainter? Beginning to fade? Perhaps, she thought, but down deep inside she knew it was more fundamental than that. Something inside her was beginning to change. Her disfigurement didn't seem quite as important any more. And if she still didn't believe she was beautiful, she was beginning to realise that she didn't mind so much any more. Maybe Lexy was right. She had been hiding from life, using her scar as an excuse to avoid really living. Well, no more.

She scouted around downstairs before she found Michelle in the farmhouse kitchen, elbow deep in flour.

'*Bonjour*, Julie. Did you sleep well?' Michelle asked, smiling warmly. 'There is *café au lait*, and bread and jam for your breakfast. Please, help yourself.'

'*Merci*,' she thanked Michelle, helping herself to a piece of crusty bread and spreading it liberally with butter and jam. 'I'm sorry I overslept—you should have woken me.'

'Pierre insisted we let you sleep. He said you have been working very hard lately, and needed the rest.' Just as Julie bit into the warm bread Pierre strode into the room.

He was wearing faded jeans and a thin black jersey. He hadn't shaved and his cheeks were rough with the beginnings of stubble. He looked completely self-assured and, Julie thought, her pulse beating rapidly, devastatingly gorgeous.

'*Ça va, Julie?*' he asked, pouring himself some coffee.

'*Oui, ca va bonne,*' she said, attempting to drag up her rusty schoolgirl French.

Michelle and Pierre exchanged a smile.

'*Ça va bien,*' Pierre corrected, grinning. 'Now it is my turn to correct you, but, please, do speak French. It suits you, and I like to hear it in that Scottish accent you have.'

'I'll try,' Julie promised. 'But perhaps when you're not around,' she countered. She didn't know what was worse, Pierre ignoring her or teasing her.

'Where's Caroline?' she asked, changing the subject.

'Still in bed. I guess she'll be happy there until lunchtime. In the meantime, I thought I could show you around.'

Julie finished her coffee with a quick gulp. 'I'd like that,' she said, wishing she could dispel the feeling of awkwardness in his company.

'We'll start in the vineyards,' Pierre said, 'then I'll show you where we make the wine.' As Julie followed Pierre outside she realised with a shiver of trepidation that it was the first time she had been alone with him since *that* night. She tried to push the memories away. If he wasn't going to bring it up, neither would she.

But it wasn't to be. As she struggled to keep up with his long strides as they made their way to the rows of vines stretching into the distance as far as the eye could see, he turned to her.

'Headache gone?' he said, a small smile tugging at the corner of his mouth. Julie felt a blush rise to the tips of her ears.

She glared at him.

'I thought we were going to pretend the other night never happened,' she said hotly. 'I had too much to drink. I'm not used to it and…' And what? She thought rapidly. It wasn't that she'd had too much to drink, only a couple of small glasses, but it was preferable to him knowing that she was unable to control her raging lust. She could hardly admit *that*. That she had kissed him back like a teenager having her first kiss.

'And…?' he prompted. If he was any sort of gentleman, Julie thought, he wouldn't be tormenting her like this. After all, he had kissed her first!

'Look,' she said, 'regardless of how you think of me, I am a woman with a normal sex drive.' She sucked in her breath. That wasn't what she had meant to say. 'I mean— Oh, dear, can't we just pretend it never happened? I promise you it won't happen again.' This time he laughed out loud. Damn the man. He was enjoying torturing her.

'*Quel dommage*—a pity.' He said. 'Never before has any woman tried to kissed me with such…honesty. It is something new for me.'

Julie was horrified. When he used the word 'honesty', did he suspect how she felt? Had he guessed how much that kiss had meant to her? Or was he implying the kiss had been awkward, lacking sophistication? She cringed inwardly. She had to make him believe it had meant nothing.

'Well, let me assure you this woman will never try to kiss you again. Honestly or otherwise.'

Suddenly Pierre's expression changed. The humour left his eyes, to be replaced with a gleam that almost made Julie step back from its intensity.

He lifted his hand and, cupping the back of her neck, pulled her towards him. She felt goose-bumps all over her body. She was powerless to resist as he drew her closer, before tilting her chin and bringing his lips down on hers.

Julie felt her whole body melt with pleasure as he explored her mouth with his tongue. She felt herself tremble as his arms swept down her back until, resting on her hips, he drew her closer into his body. She gasped with pleasure as warmth flooded her body and she felt time stand still. This is where I belong. That was her last thought as she gave in to his kisses and pressed her body into his.

It could have been seconds, minutes or hours before they drew apart. Pierre gazed down at her, looking stunned. He dropped his hands to his sides, his fists clenching and un-clenching. '*Merde*,' he said, his voice hoarse. Julie held his look, drowning in his silver eyes. So this is what I've been missing all my life, she thought blissfully.

Pierre opened his mouth as if he was about to say something when they heard shouts coming from the field lower down. Pierre and Julie looked at each other. It was clear that some-thing had happened. As one they started moving quickly in the direction of the shouts. As they ran, Julie could see a tractor in the distance, beside which two men were calling and gesticu-lating, clearly agitated. As soon as they approached the tractor they could see the cause of the commotion. Alain was lying on the ground, holding a mutilated hand and crying out in anguish. Next to him another man was kneeling, attempting to stem the blood spurting from his arm with the pressure of his hands. Julie didn't need to follow the rapid French exchange between the man and Pierre to realise what had happened. Somehow Alain's hand had become trapped in the machinery attached to the tractor. The sharp blades had lacerated his hand to such an extent that Julie doubted it was salvageable. At least he wasn't trapped any longer, Julie thought as she took in the scene. Pierre was taking command of the situation.

'Julie, run back to the house and ask Michelle for the emer-gency kit. And ice and a plastic bag. Then ask her to phone for an ambulance. Try and keep her calm.'

Julie spun on her heal and sprinted the several hundred metres back to the house. She paused outside the kitchen to catch her breath. She needed Michelle's co-operation if they were to help Alain.

Michelle was shocked and distressed, but pointed Julie in the direction of the emergency kit before picking up the phone to call for help. Julie only had time to give her a reassuring squeeze on the shoulder before she was off again. Her return trip was slower, the heavy bag impeding her progress. By the time she arrived back, Pierre had elevated the injured limb and appeared to have stopped the bleeding. There was so much blood, Julie thought. He'll go into shock soon if we don't do something. She opened the medical bag, hugely relieved to find there was a line and a bag of fluids that Pierre obviously kept for emergencies such as these. Quickly she tore open the giving set and inserted the needle into one of Alain's veins. At the same time Pierre was attaching the bag of saline to the tube in Alain's arm. Julie and Pierre worked together as naturally as if they'd been doing so for years and Pierre continued to speak soothingly to Alain throughout. Although his eyes were closed, Alain seemed calm. Julie could only wonder at his fortitude. He must be terrified as well as in the most awful pain. But at least they had morphine to give him, Julie thought as she drew up a dose and injected it into another of Alain's veins. It wasn't as big a dose as she would have liked to have given him, but until they had him in hospital it was the best she could do. Having done that, she examined his injured hand closely. She was shocked to realise that although the injury to his hand wasn't as bad as she had thought, three of his fingers had been sliced off.

In the distance she could hear the wail of the ambulance. Michelle came running towards them, her apron flying behind her. She dropped to her knees beside her husband, crying and murmuring words of endearment. She looked up at Pierre, her eyes saying all she needed to.

He spoke to her in French. Julie could understand enough to know he was telling Michelle that Alain would be all right, but they needed to get him to hospital. He said something about fingers and slipped something into the plastic bag of ice, before handing it to Julie. As she took the bag from him she realised that while she had been away he had found the severed fingers and had hopes of reattaching them. But surely it was possible only if they got Alain to hospital quickly?

The ambulance, following the tracks of the tractor, made its agonisingly slow way towards them. Eventually it was close enough for them, with the help of the paramedics, to load Alain in. Pierre jumped in beside his friend, shaking his head at Michelle. 'I'm sorry, *chérie*,' he said in French. 'You must follow us in the car.' As the paramedic was pulling the doors closed behind them, he added, 'Julie, can you drive Michelle to the hospital? She will show you where to go. Take my car.' And then the doors closed and, with the siren back on, the ambulance sped off.

Julie and Michelle hurried back to the house where they met Caroline, looking bewildered and panic-stricken.

'What's going on? What on earth's wrong?' she asked, her eyes darting from woman to woman. 'Someone's been hurt, haven't they? Who is it? Are they all right? Is it Pierre?' she gripped Julie's arm. 'Tell me, please.'

'Alain's hurt, but he's going to be all right. I'll tell you about it later, but Michelle and I need to go to the hospital. Pierre has gone with Alain in the ambulance. He said we should follow in his car. Where are the keys?'

Caroline reached behind her, lifting as set of keys from the hook behind the door. 'We'll take Alain and Michelle's car. Pierre's only holds two and I'm coming with you.'

It took an excruciating thirty minutes before they arrived at the hospital. Apart from a brief explanation to Caroline as to what had happened, the women were silent. Although Julie suspected that Pierre was going to attempt to sew the severed fingers back on, she didn't want to say anything to Michelle prior to discussing it with him. Perhaps there had been too long a delay; perhaps there weren't the necessary facilities at the country hospital. At this point, apart from reassuring Michelle that Alain would be all right there was little else she could say without the danger of falsely raising her hopes.

The three women dashed into the accident and emergency department. The head nurse prevented Michelle and Caroline from going beyond the doors of the resus room, but allowed Julie in. 'Dr Favatier said you were to be shown in as soon as you arrived,' she said in accented but otherwise perfect English. 'He plans to operate and attempt to reattach the fingers. He said you are to assist. Once you have spoken to the doctor, I shall get someone to take you along to theatre. We only have one Theatre but luckily there is no one else needing it at the moment so he can go straight in.'

Well, Julie thought wryly, I am certainly getting to Pierre work in his home country—just not in the circumstances I hoped for.

Alain was lying on the gurney, a temporary dressing on his injured arm. He looked groggy but comfortable. Pierre was in conversation with another medic and a nurse. Probably discussing the operation, Julie surmised.

'Is it okay if Michelle comes in for a few minutes?' Julie asked. 'I think she needs to see for herself that Alain is all right.'

'Of course,' Pierre said, barely glancing at her.

He had already changed into theatre scrubs. Seeing him in hospital gear, with the different more authoritative persona he seemed to adopt whenever he was working, Julie felt herself distanced from him and was reminded forcibly of their professional relationship. Was he already regretting the kiss? This time there was no doubt in her mind. He had kissed her as if he had meant it. Why, then, did she feel a chill run down her spine? But she had to remember he was desperately worried.

'I'll go and fetch her and explain what we are planning to do,' he said. 'We will be taking him into Theatre in about ten minutes. ' He turned his attention back to Alain, saying something that Julie couldn't follow but which made the injured man smile weakly.

Julie turned to the nurse who had shown her in. 'I'll go up to Theatre now and get scrubbed if you could show me where to go.'

The operation took until the afternoon. Julie assisted as Pierre, who used a powerful microscope to magnify the field, carefully reattached first the severed blood vessels then the nerves of the missing fingers with microscopic stitches. His concentration was complete. Not once did Julie see him waver as worked. Throughout the operation he explained to her exactly what he was doing and telling her patiently how she needed to assist him. Although concerned for Alain, Julie found the whole procedure fascinating, and as before she found she was able to anticipate Pierre's movements. At last, the operation complete, he stood back from the table and stretched luxuriously.

'*Alors!*' he said, clearly satisfied. 'Now it is in the lap of the gods but, given the way his fingers are pinking up, at least the blood supply has returned. We shall have to wait until we can tell how much use of the fingers he will retain. The next few days will be critical.' As he peeled off his mask and gloves, Julie could see tiredness wash over him. Whatever he showed outwardly, God knew what reserves he needed to concentrate for such long periods of time. Julie also guessed that the fact that Alain was his friend added to tension of the procedure. 'I shall go and speak to Michelle,' he said. 'Then I think you should take them home. Once Alain comes round from the anaesthetic he will sleep. Probably until the morning.'

But Michelle, although relieved that the procedure had gone well, refused to leave her husband's side. Pierre also insisted on staying until his friend had come round from the anaesthetic. 'Take Caroline home, please, Julie,' he asked. 'Tell everyone that the operation went as well as could be expected.'

'What about you?' Julie asked. 'How will you get back?' She looked directly into his eyes, wanting some connection with him. Wanting to know that back there in the vineyard had meant something to him too. Surely this time she couldn't have been mistaken?

'I'll find someone to give me a lift home. Don't worry, I know them all well here. I used to come here to help out when I was a medical student and still operate here when they need me.' He must have seen the questioning look in her eyes. 'We'll talk later, Julie,' he said. 'First I have to make sure Alain is okay.'

Reluctantly, Julie left Pierre and Michelle to their bedside vigil. Unbidden, an image of Pierre, feet up on a coffee-table, flirting with one of the gorgeous French nurses, leapt into her mind. She pushed the thought away, horrified to discover how jealous the thought made her. As she drove a subdued Caroline back to the house, her mind wandered back to the kiss she and

Pierre had shared. She couldn't believe it hadn't meant something to him. Nobody could kiss a woman like that without caring for her—even a little. She thought back to the feel of his lips on hers, the feel of his lean body, hard against hers. His fingers on the back of her neck. She almost moaned aloud. Damn, damn damn, she cursed inwardly. Despite her best intentions, she had done the very thing every fibre of her being had warned her against doing. She had fallen in love with Dr Pierre Favatier. But how did he feel about her?

As they were pulling up in front of the farm house after a silent journey, Caroline finally spoke.

'Something bad always seems to happen here. I hate it. I want to go back home.'

Julie looked at her sympathetically. Being here, the place where her parents had spent their last few days, must be hard. Instead of bringing some closure to the young woman, it seemed to remind her of everything she had lost.

'We can go back any time you like,' she said softly. 'You can stay with me until your uncle returns.'

'Could we? Could I?' Caroline said, sounding relieved. She grasped Julie's hand. 'Thank you. I don't know why you put up with me—you don't owe us anything yet you want to help us.'

But Julie knew that Caroline was rapidly becoming the younger sister she'd never had. And it didn't have anything to do with the fact she was Pierre's niece. It was probably something to do with the loneliness she knew the young woman felt. It was the same feeling she'd had for years.

She smiled at Caroline. 'Hey, I like you. I think we have stuff in common.'

As they got out of the car, Caroline looked at Julie specu-

latively. 'Nothing to do with Uncle Pierre, then?' Julie drew
a sharp breath. Had she guessed how Julie felt? Before Julie
could formulate a reply, Caroline continued. 'I'm sorry. I
shouldn't have said that. I know you aren't that sort of person.'
By this time they were in the kitchen. Caroline sat at the
table, absent-mindedly tracing the deep grooves in the wood
while Julie tipped some milk into a saucepan to heat.

'Anyway, I don't think he's your type.'

Julie was loath to get into a conversation with Caroline
about Pierre, but she was couldn't help feel stung.

'I'm not his type, you mean.' She tried a laugh but even to
her ears it sounded hollow.

'No, you're not...' Caroline said slowly. 'Papa used to say
that Pierre liked them tall, beautiful and brainless. And
you're...' She clasped a hand over her mouth.

'Not too tall, not beautiful and...'

'Not brainless,' Caroline finished for her, and the two
women laughed. Julie poured the hot milk into two mugs and
added a liberal amount of hot chocolate that she'd found in
one of the cupboards. She sat down next to Caroline.

'But, actually, I think he does like you,' Caroline went on.

Julie felt her cheeks grow warm.

'I hope he does like me,' she said, deliberately misunder-
standing the younger woman's meaning. 'He's my boss. I
have to keep on the right side of him.'

'No. It's more than that. It's the way he looks at you. You
make him smile.' Julie felt her heart beating in her chest. Could
Caroline be right? Did Pierre feel something for her? Was she
more to him than just a colleague and a friend to his niece?

She stood as Caroline yawned. 'C'mon,' she said, clearing
the cups from the table. 'I think it's time for bed.'

But after Caroline had gone up, Julie felt too restless to follow suit. Instead, she made herself a cup of coffee and, slipping into her coat, took her drink onto the large veranda that surrounded the house.

As she sipped her drink, she mulled over the day's events. She kept coming back to the feel of Pierre's arms around her and the pressure of his lips on hers. She'd had a few dates since Luke, but none of them had ever sparked the feelings within her that Pierre had. Not remotely.

She looked out over the vineyards, the early spring breeze rustling the leaves on the trees. The moon was full, casting a silver glow as far as the eye could see. For the first time in as long as she could remember Julie felt at peace. She loved it here, she thought, and thinking back to that moment amongst the vines before they had been interrupted, she knew with breathtaking clarity that she loved Pierre. Loved him completely, hopelessly and for ever. But how did he feel about her? Was it really possible that he felt something in return? Or was she, as she suspected, about to have her heart broken?

CHAPTER EIGHT

JULIE was interrupted from her musings by the arrival of a car. She watched as Pierre with a few words in French to the driver and climbed out. As he came towards her she caught his look of surprise. Damn it! Did he think she had been waiting for him, ready to take up where they had left off in the vineyard? But weren't you secretly hoping for that? an unwelcome voice whispered in her ear.

'You are still awake, then?' he said.

He sat down on the bench on the veranda and stretched his long legs in front of him. He had changed back into his jeans and T-shirt and even in the half-light Julie could make out the lines of tiredness around his mouth and eyes. Once again she felt every fibre of her being react to his presence. Each individual nerve in her body seemed to be straining towards him. She longed to pull him close, kiss the lines of worry from his mouth and soothe the lines of tiredness from his eyes. But something in his expression stopped her.

'I couldn't sleep. Caroline has gone up, though. How is Alain?'

'He is all right. We'll know more in the morning. Michelle insisted on spending the night with him. She wants to be there when he wakes up.' Julie didn't know if it were tiredness, or whether it was because Pierre was back on his native soil, but his accent seemed more pronounced. He had never seemed more French to her—or more distant.

'But I am glad you are still awake,' he said. 'I wanted to talk to you. There is something I have to tell you.'

The flatness in his voice chilled Julie.

She turned away from him and looked out across the fields. She suspected she wasn't going to want to hear whatever it was he had to say.

'Julie, look at me,' he said softly. Reluctantly she turned until she was facing him. The air seemed to cool and Julie shivered, wrapping her arms around herself.

'I'm sorry,' Pierre said. 'I shouldn't have kissed you before. In your flat. And then again in the vineyard. I had no right.'

'It was only a kiss!' She tried to keep her voice light. 'Men and women kiss all the time without it meaning anything.'

'But you're not the kind of woman to kiss a man without it meaning something. Are you?' he said softly, and Julie could hear something—could it be regret?—in his voice.

'No,' she admitted softly.

'Then it was not right. I should not have done it. I must tell you—I can't love another woman. You have to know that.'

'Katherine?' Julie said, icy tendrils creeping through her veins.

Pierre hesitated.

'Not Katherine,' he said at last. 'Iona.'

'Iona? Caroline's mother?' So her suspicions had been right! It all made sense. The way he had looked at the photograph. The way he had said his sister-in law's name when he had woken up that day in her flat.

'You were in love with your brother's wife?'

'I was always in love with her—from the first time I met her. And if it wasn't for me, she'd still be alive.'

Julie looked at him. Gone was the smiling, sophisticated surgeon. Instead, standing before her was a man who looked as if he had lost everything. She felt her throat tighten.

'Did she love you?' The words came before she could stop them. Her head was reeling.

He looked bleak.

'Once—perhaps. But by the time I realised I loved her it was too late. She had met my brother and fallen in love with him.'

'Did she know how you felt?'

'Yes. She guessed. Eventually. After Caroline was born.' He said harshly, 'I wasn't as good at hiding my feelings as I thought. That's why she left France.' Julie could hear the pain in his voice. 'She believed it was for the best. That once we were separated by hundreds of miles I'd get over her.'

'And did you?' Julie breathed, her heart growing cold.

'No,' he said, his voice flat. 'I will always love her. There will never be anyone else for me. Every time I look at Caroline it is Iona's face I see. Sometimes it is almost more than I can bear.'

His words stabbed into Julie's heart like a thousand needles. She loved him. She knew it with devastating clarity. The way she felt about him was the way a woman felt only once in a lifetime—if she was very lucky. But it was no use. He had made it clear that there was no room for her in his life. She had given him a glimpse of her heart and he had turned away from her.

Now, more than ever before, Julie knew she had to hide the way she felt from Pierre.

'It was just a couple of kisses,' she said again, struggling to keep her voice light. 'We are both adults. Let's not read more into it than it was.'

Something moved behind Pierre's eyes. Was it relief? Regret? Julie couldn't be sure, but given what he had just told her it was far more likely to be relief.

'You are a beautiful person.' He tapped his chest. 'Here inside where it really matters.' Julie couldn't help but smile at the theatrical gesture.

'Ah, beautiful inside,' she said softly. 'The equivalent of saying we should be friends.'

Pierre looked puzzled. 'I mean it. You are lovely inside and out. You give so much to other people…' He stood and stepped towards her. Instinctively, Julie moved away from him until her back was pressing against the railings of the veranda. It was taking all her self-control not to let him see how much she was hurting. If he came any closer, she was in danger of breaking down.

Pierre stood over her. The moon slipped behind a cloud and for a moment his expression was hidden from her. In the darkness she could feel his presence. The air seemed to snap and crackle between them. Surely he wasn't as indifferent to her as he was making out? She felt his finger trace the scar on her cheek. He said something in rapid French that Julie couldn't follow. Then with a muttered oath he stepped away from her.

'You must believe in yourself. One day you will find someone who loves you—only you. Someone who sees how beautiful you are who will make you believe it.'

'How I feel about myself has nothing to do with you. You have made that clear,' Julie said, beginning to get angry. Who was he to tell her what she should and should not be feeling? And how patronising to tell her she would find someone who would love her. If he didn't want her, that was one thing, but to wish her on someone else. How *dared* he? 'And if you're worried about a repetition of today's events, don't be. It won't happen again. Caroline and I are going back to Scotland tomorrow.'

'Tomorrow? Does she hate it here so much? Does she hate me so much? And you?'

'It's not all about you, Pierre,' Jules said hotly. 'Caroline is finding it difficult to be here where her parents spent their last few days. Surely you can understand that? And she senses that being around her makes you unhappy. She thinks you are angry with her.'

Pierre's eyes turned as bleak as a winter morning. 'I have failed her, when all I wanted was to protect Iona's daughter. I hoped that being here, where her papa grew up, where her parents were so happy for a time, would help,' Pierre said. He chewed on his lip. 'I was wrong to bring her. It is too soon.'

'And for you?' Julie asked. 'How do you feel, being here?'

Pierre looked away and Julie felt her heart crack as she saw a spasm of pain twist his mouth.

'I kept away when they were here,' he said. 'I had my work, my home in Paris. I knew it would be too hard seeing them here together so much in love.'

'Is that why you never went to see them in Scotland?' Julie asked. She didn't want to hear, but she couldn't help wanting to share his pain.

'Yes. I was selfish—I can see that now. Jacques never understood why I avoided him and his family. Why I never took the time to see them. In France family is important. But I guess he put it down to my selfish ways. And it was easier to let him think that.'

'Poor Caroline,' Julie said. 'I'm sure part of the reason she is so angry with you is that she doesn't understand why you neglected your family.'

'If I had gone to see them, if I had put my own feelings aside, maybe they wouldn't have died. They would have stayed in Scotland and been safe. Caroline is right to blame me.'

'That's just ridiculous.' Julie said hotly. 'It was an accident. A tragic, terrible accident. You can't possibly hold yourself responsible.'

'But I do,' Pierre softly. 'And I must somehow find a way to make it right with Caroline. I need to make sure she is happy. I owe her parents that, at least.'

'Then you need to start by trying to talk to her,' Julie said. 'She needs to know that you love her—not just that you feel a duty towards her.'

'Why are you so wise? And you not much older than my niece?' Pierre said with a small smile.

But I'm not so bloody wise, Julie wanted to say, otherwise I wouldn't have fallen for you. But, of course, she couldn't say the words. He had made it perfectly clear that whatever he felt for her wasn't, and would never be, love. All at once the fight went out of her. Let him do as he pleased. He and his family were no concern of hers. However much she wished they were.

'I think I'll go to bed,' she said through stiff lips. Avoiding his eyes, so he wouldn't see how much she was hurting, she left him alone, staring into the night.

Pierre stayed on the veranda for a few moments, thinking about what Julie had said. He knew she had been telling him the truth. He had been so wrapped up in his own grief he hadn't really given the girl upstairs as much thought as he should have. The truth was that she looked so much like Iona and Jacques, it almost tore his heart apart. But Julie was right. It was about time he thought about his niece instead of his own pain. He had been unbelievably selfish. And what was almost worse, he had hurt the very person who had tried to help him. He closed his eyes against the image of Julie's dark grey eyes awash with pain. He groaned. He had been a selfish fool. Seeking comfort when he had nothing to give in return.

He went upstairs and looked inside the bedroom in which Caroline was sleeping. But to his consternation he found it empty. Where was she? Then a thought struck him. He moved along the dark passageway towards the room that he and his brother had shared as children. The one Iona and Jacques had slept in the night before their deaths. He had only been in it once since then, but had found it, with its faint scent of Iona's perfume, too painful to visit again. He opened the door and, sure enough, sitting on the bed, clutching a teddy that had belonged to his brother when he'd been a child, sat Caroline, who was sobbing as if her heart would break.

He strode over to her and gathered the stricken teenager in his arms. 'Shh, *mon chou*,' he said, rocking her gently. 'It is all right. It is all going to be all right.'

After some time her sobs quietened until he felt her relax in his arms. He brushed her hair out of her swollen eyes.

'I miss them so much, Pierre,' Caroline whispered. 'Why did they have to die? It's so unfair.'

'I know,' he said. 'If I could have died in their place I would have.'

'Why didn't you come and see us?' Caroline asked, looking up at him with eyes in which he could see her terrible pain.

'Papa missed you so much. And Mama too. I heard him telling her that he couldn't understand why you didn't come.'

'And what did she say?' he asked quietly.

'She said she was sure you had your reasons. That she knew you loved us, but life wasn't always as simple as we wanted it to be.'

'She was a good woman,' Pierre said. 'Your father was lucky to be married to her.'

Caroline looked at him sharply. 'And she was lucky to be married to him. She was always telling him that she was glad she had married the right brother. What did she mean?' Pierre felt a sliver of pain run through his heart. Perhaps it was best he told Caroline the truth, however painful he found it.

'I don't know if she ever told you, but your mother was my girlfriend first.' He could tell by Caroline's frown that this was news to her.

'I met her in Paris when I was a medical student and she was working as an au pair. I—we—fell in love. But I was young and not ready to settle down.'

'Did she love you?' Caroline asked.

'I think she thought she was in love with me. Then I brought her here to meet my family and she met your papa. Straight away she fell in love with him.'

'How did you feel about that? Did you mind?'

'Yes, I minded very much. As soon as I knew she was lost to me, I realised that I did love her—with all my heart. But it was too late.'

'Did Papa know?'

'No, I never really realised it myself until I saw them together, and once I knew the truth there was no point in telling him how I felt. They were so happy together I knew that whatever feelings she'd had for me were nothing to the way she felt about him.'

'It must have been hard for you.'

'The day the got married was one of the saddest, and happiest, days of my life. I was sad because I knew I had lost the woman I loved for good, but happy because I knew that she and your father were meant for each other, and that they would make each other happy.'

'Did she know you were in love with her?'

'I never told her, but I think she guessed. It is why they only came here when I wasn't here, and why I never came to see you. I did see you once. Do you remember when your *grand-père* died? Seeing you was almost as hard for me as the day they married. You looked—look—so much like her. Every time I see you…'

'You are reminded of her,' Caroline finished for him. She sat deep in thought, remaining in her uncle's embrace. 'Poor Pierre. Is that why you never married?'

'I never did meet a woman who made me feel the way your mother made me feel. I didn't want to. If I couldn't be with her, I didn't want to be with anyone. Not permanently anyway.'

'You know, it makes me feel better somehow. That Mama had two men who loved her. She was lucky. But I was so angry with you. If you had come to see them, they wouldn't have been in that plane in France.'

'I know, *ma chérie*. I blame myself too. But they needed to be here. They wanted to see the lawyers—they had papers to sign.'

'About the vineyard? They didn't really talk to me much about it.'

'Yes. It was to do with a trust they wanted set up for you.

I would probably found an excuse to stay in Paris if I hadn't had to sign papers, too.'

'And you never married because you loved Mama?'

'I'm afraid so,' Pierre admitted.

'But what about Julie?' Caroline asked, looking at Pierre intently.

'What about her?'

'I've seen the way you are when she's around. You're different. Happy. And the way you look at her, it's the way Mama used to look at Papa.'

Pierre was stunned. The way he looked at Julie? Of course he liked her, found her attractive. Very attractive. And sexy and amusing, and clever and thoughtful and very good company. All of these things he admitted. But being in love with Iona had never stopped him desiring other women. Even if he'd known it would only be a matter of time before he tired of them. But Julie? He wouldn't sleep with her, no matter how much he wanted to. Because he knew she would never take any relationship lightly and he was too fond of her—he owed her too much—to hurt her. He had hurt her enough as it was. No, Caroline was wrong. He wanted Julie, but anything else was all in his niece's imagination. Wasn't it?

'But I'm glad you told me about Mama,' Caroline said sleepily. 'I don't know why, but it makes me feel better.' She got to her feet. 'I think I'll go to bed now. And I think I'll tell Julie I don't want to go back to Scotland just yet. I'd like to spend some more time here, where they were both so happy. And maybe you and I can get to know each other properly.'

Pierre sat deep in thought long after Caroline had returned to her room. Was she right? Was he falling for Julie? Had Iona's death in some way allowed him to move on with his life? Had that been her last gift to him? To allow him at last to find someone who he could love and who would love him in return? Eventually he rose and went back to his own room.

As he lay in bed later that night, he tossed and turned. Whenever he closed his eyes it was Julie he saw. He saw her luminous eyes, the pain she tried to hide, the wounded curve to her mouth. What was it about her that seemed to have got under his skin? She was different from the woman he usually dated—she had a depth to her that he avoided.

His thoughts drifted back to Iona, who was never far from his mind. But instead of the usual pang of terrible grief that her memory usually evoked, this time he felt only sadness that her life had been so tragically cut short. Giving up on sleep, he got out of bed and, pulling on his jeans and sweater, let himself out of the house. He made his way down to the small lake at the back of the house, to the place he had first kissed Iona when he had brought her here all these years ago. He stood beside the lake, remembering the feel of her lips and the scent of her hair, but this time it was other eyes he was seeing. Smoky grey eyes with a hint of sadness. Could it be that he was no longer in love with Iona? He had believed himself in love with her for so long it had become a habit. But perhaps he had convinced himself as a way of keeping other women at arm's length? Surely if he had truly loved the woman his brother had married, he would never have let her go? Instead, he had introduced her to Jacques, and had never fought for her.

With a sense of wonder Pierre realised that since he had met Julie he had thought less and less of the woman who had become his sister-in-law. He was beginning to realise that he had used the belief he was in love with her as a barrier against allowing other women into his heart. He had been scared of commitment, he realised. Scared of risking having his heart broken. Until Julie had come along, that was. She had crept under his skin and into his heart. The thought shocked him. It was her face that slid into his dreams, her mouth he dreamt of. Her arms he wanted around him at night. Stunned, he looked over the lake. It was Julie he wanted by his side, here, in France, with him. For ever. And he couldn't wait to see her to tell her.

Julie woke just as the light was beginning to leak through her curtains. She felt a momentary pang of sadness as she remembered that she'd be leaving the vineyard later that day. But perhaps it was just as well. No matter how much she wanted to, she'd never belong here.

She showered quickly, before making her way to the deserted kitchen. A couple of used bowls lay on the table, telling her that she wasn't the first person to breakfast. She poured herself a cup of coffee and went to stand on the veranda to drink it. The sun was rising and although it was still early spring, Julie could feel the first hint of summer in the breeze.

In the distance she could see a solitary figure down by the vineyards. She recognised the jet-black hair and tall figure of Pierre. What should she do? she thought. Stay away or pretend that nothing happened? Sighing, she made up her mind. She'd be leaving soon. She may as well face him sooner rather than later. He was more likely to believe that his kisses had meant nothing if she behaved normally. She grabbed a blanket and wrapped some crusty bread in a napkin. Then, taking her coffee with her, she made her way towards him. As she approached she could see that he had removed his shirt. He seemed to be tying the branches of the vines, and as he worked she could see his bronzed muscles ripple. She felt a sudden wash of desire.

'Coffee,' she said as she approached.

He accepted her offer, taking a long drink before returning to his work.

'I thought I would get some of this done before the rest of the men arrive,' he explained. 'Then I can honestly tell Alain we are making progress when I go to see him later.'

'Can I help?' Julie offered. 'I don't know what time we have to leave for the airport, but I'm happy to do what I can in the meantime,' she said, trying to keep her eyes off his naked torso.

'Caroline doesn't want to go back any more,' Pierre answered. 'She's decided to stay after all.'

'That's good,' Julie said, surprised. 'But what made her change her mind?'

'I talked to her last night. As you suggested,' he replied.

'Oh,' Julie said, wondering what Pierre had said that had convinced his niece to stay.

'Can I assume you will stay, too?' Pierre asked. Something in the expression in his eyes as he looked at her made Julie's pulse race.

'I think I should go back. It sounds as if you don't need me here any more.'

'But we want you to stay,' Pierre replied, looking steadily at Julie. 'I want you to stay.'

Julie could hear a pounding in her ears. The way he was looking at her. The urgent note in his voice. It seemed different. He seemed different. Suddenly her throat was dry.

'Of course I'll stay, then,' she said. 'I love it here. It's so peaceful. I have to back at work on Wednesday but until then I'm all yours.'

'All mine?' Pierre said softly. 'Is that so?'

He took the blanket from her hands and laid it on the ground. The way he was looking at her sent waves of desire through Julie. Confused, she was powerless to react when Pierre took her hand and pulled her down beside him.

He stretched himself along the length of the blanket, shielding his eyes with his arm. Julie had to fight to stop herself from reaching out to touch the contours of his bronzed muscular chest. She was conscious of trying to imprint the image of him on her memory.

'After the harvest, we usually have a party,' he said lazily. 'All the workers who have helped, as well as the surrounding families, come. We party into the night.'

'It sounds fun,' Julie said. Once again miserably aware she wouldn't be part of it.

'And what do you do for fun?' he asked. 'You seem to spend so much of it looking after other people. Your work, your friends you look after, us. But what about Julie, what does she want?'

'I have everything I want,' Julie said softly. 'I love my work and the kids. I have friends, my skiing. My life is full.'

'Why do you not seem happy, then? When I look at you there is sometimes—*Je ne sais pas*—a sadness.'

Julie felt uncomfortable. She wasn't used to talking about herself and she had already revealed too much of herself to this man.

'I am happy,' she said defensively.

Pierre reached out and stroked her arm, his roughened fingers sending sparks of desire through Julie.

'But I don't think you are. Sometimes I see you smile, even laugh. But not very often. I think you are more sad than happy.'

Julie pulled away from his touch. 'I don't need your sympathy,' she said sharply.

Pierre looked puzzled, then his face brightened. 'I don't feel sorry for you! *Merde*, you are not the sort of woman a man feels sorry for.'

She looked into his eyes. Flickering in the depths she could see something. Desire? Passion? Or was he simply poking fun at her?

Before she could decide she was in his arms. He pulled her down onto the blanket so close she could feel the heat and hardness of his naked chest. Unable to help herself, she felt her arms snake around his neck. Then he was kissing her his lips, hard and demanding. She responded, letting herself lean into his body. She could feel his arms around her waist then on her hips, drawing her into him. She could feel the heat of her desire deep in her belly. She hadn't made love to anyone before and she felt a terrifying mixture of fear and need. Then the world disappeared and all she was conscious of was her desire. It didn't matter that he would never love her. All she wanted at this moment was him. To stay in his arms for ever.

His hands were on her, undoing her buttons of her blouse. She felt his touch on her naked breasts and she arched her body into his. Then she was being lifted as if she were a baby. Still kissing her, he carried her back towards the house and up the stairs. She knew what he intended, but she was powerless to stop him. She didn't want to stop him. He kicked open the door of his bedroom and laid her gently on the bed. He looked at her for a few seconds. Now there was no mistaking the strength of his desire. His eyes drilled into hers.

'I want you,' he said simply. 'I need you, but I need to be sure that you want this too. Because if I touch you again, will not be able to stop.'

Julie looked up at him. Her breath was coming in short gasps. Her body felt as if it was on fire. Whatever happened in the future she knew she wanted him right now more than anything else in the world. Unable to speak the words, she reached out for him and, grabbing the belt around his waist, pulled him on top of her.

Later, much later, they lay together, the rumpled sheets caught in their limbs. Julie's head was on Pierre's chest and he stroked her hair gently before trailing his fingers across her face, stopping briefly at her scar before moving towards her neck. But for the first time Julie didn't flinch at the acknowledgement of her disfigurement. It just didn't matter any more. Now, at last, she believed herself beautiful. As she listened to the steady beating of his heart, she opened her eyes and glanced around his room. She wanted to know everything about this man. Every detail, going back to his babyhood. She smiled to herself, finding it difficult to imagine the six-foot man beside her had ever been a baby.

His room was the mirror image of hers, but instead of pillows and cushions it was simple and masculine, containing the bed they were in, an old-fashioned wardrobe and a chest of drawers. Apart from those items of furniture, the room was bare.

'Julie,' Pierre said, his voice low and wondering. 'You were a virgin?'

'Yes,' she said simply. 'There has never been anyone. When I was with Luke we were too young—well, I was. And since him there has never been anyone I felt strongly enough about to sleep with.'

'But me, you felt strongly enough about me?' He tipped

her face up so she was forced to look in his eyes. She felt suddenly shy. But she wasn't the sort of woman to play games. She couldn't pretend that what had just happened hadn't meant something.

'Yes,' she said again. 'I have never felt this way about anyone.'

Pierre picked up her hand and turning it over kissed her palm.

'Then you must marry me,' he said. 'And soon.'

Julie felt a surge of happiness flow through her body. He loved her. Despite what he'd said about Iona. He wanted her to be with him always. She turned her face up to his. He was smiling down at her. It was all so sudden…

'Don't make me wait for your answer,' he growled. 'You must know by now that I am not a patient man.'

'Then yes, my darling. Yes.' And then he was kissing her and she was drowning once more.

Julie must have fallen asleep because when she opened her eyes Pierre was getting dressed. He bent down and kissed her, but when she reached for him he pulled away with a regretful smile. 'Later, *mon coeur*,' he said. 'Stay here if you want, but I have to go to the hospital to see Alain. There will be time later—tonight.' His eyes glittered as he looked down at her. 'If only you knew how much I want to stay with you, but there will be plenty of time for us.' His eyes glowed with promise and Julie felt her body stir with desire. She stretched luxuriously. God, had she known what she had been missing all these years! But at the same time she was glad she had waited.

'Don't be too long,' she said.

When she next awoke a glance at her watch told her it was almost lunchtime. She jumped out of bed. Caroline would be looking for her, and she wasn't ready to be found naked in Pierre's bed. She wanted a few more hours to hug the secret of her engagement to herself. As she dressed she felt her heart sing. She would be with Pierre the rest of their lives. They could spend their free time here at the vineyard. And when they had children… She stopped midway through getting dressed. Did Pierre want children? She hoped so because she wanted three at least. Anyway, there would be time to discuss all that. But she couldn't imagine Pierre not wanting kids. She let herself daydream. Three children, two boys and a girl or two girls and a boy. She didn't care. Hell, three boys, three girls as long as they were healthy and had Pierre's blue eyes and dark hair.

Humming happily to herself, she went downstairs. She met Caroline at the door of the kitchen. The girl looked upset.

'Hey, Caroline. What is it? Is there news of Alain? Has something happened?' Fear clenched her throat. She barely knew Alain or his wife, but already she was fond of them.

Caroline shook her head. She held out her hand to Julie. In it she was holding Julie's mobile phone.

'It kept ringing. I couldn't find you, so I answered it. It's the hospice in Edinburgh. They want to speak to you about your friend Lexy.'

Her heart beating rapidly in her chest, Julie took the phone from Caroline. Please, God, she thought, let her still be alive.

'Hello,' she said, her voice shaky.

'Julie, it's Audrey. I'm so sorry to track you down like this, but you said you wanted to know if Lexy took a turn for the worse. Well, I'm sorry to have to tell you she had a small stroke last night and she's fading fast. She's asking for you.'

'How long has she got?' Julie asked, her throat dry.

'Not long,' Audrey replied gently. 'A day or two at the most.'

'Tell her I'll be there as soon as I can. I'll get the first flight possible.'

'I'm sorry, Julie,' Caroline said slowly as Julie ended the call. 'Is it your friend at the hospice?'

Julie nodded. She needed to get back. To see her before... She couldn't bear to think about it. Although she had always known it was only ever a matter of time before Lexy succumbed to her illness, she wasn't ready to let her friend go. Besides, she wanted to see her, to reassure her that she had at last found the happiness that Lexy so desperately wanted for her.

Seeing that Julie was shocked and distressed, Caroline took command. 'I'll call the airport. Book you on a flight. You get packed. Where's Pierre? I'm sure he'll be happy to drive you to the airport.'

'He's at the hospital. With Alain and Michelle. Please, don't disturb him. I can get a taxi. If I can get a flight today.' Julie turned on her heel and sped up the stairs. She started throwing her clothes into her suitcase. After a few minutes Caroline appeared to tell her that she had managed to find her a seat on a plane that was leaving in two hours. Caroline had also called her a taxi, which was on its way. It would give Julie just enough time to get to the airport if she hurried.

She had just enough time to finish packing when the taxi announced its arrival with a blast on its horn. Although she knew it was unlikely, Julie had hoped that Pierre would be back in time for her to at least say goodbye. But he wasn't back and Julie couldn't risk waiting even a few minutes. Not if she wanted to be certain of catching the plane.

'Tell Pierre goodbye for me,' she told Caroline as she

kissed her farewell. 'I'll see you both in Edinburgh at the weekend.' And then with a final brief hug she was in the taxi and heading towards the airport. Julie didn't know whether it was worry about Lexy or something else, but as she watched the farm recede from the rear window of the taxi, she felt an shiver of dread.

It was almost nine in the evening by the time the plane touched down in Edinburgh. Julie jumped in another taxi and headed straight for the hospice. She didn't want to waste precious minutes stopping at her flat.

She rushed inside St Margaret's, almost colliding with the late-shift nurses going off duty.

Arriving at Lexy's ward, she stopped at the nurses' station. Audrey was putting on her coat about to leave.

'That was quick.' She looked at Julie in surprise. 'I didn't think you'd be here until tomorrow morning at the earliest.'

'How is she?' Julie asked, praying that she wasn't too late.

'She's holding her own. I think she's hanging on until she sees you.'

'Can I go in?' Julie asked.

'Of course,' Audrey replied. 'She's drifting in and out of consciousness. Sometimes she's lucid—other times she seems to be back in the 1940s.'

Julie crept into Lexy's room.

Her friend had her eyes closed and Julie was shocked by how she seemed to have shrunk since she'd last seen her. Her face was almost as white as the sheets on which she lay, her eyes hollow and surrounded by deep dark circles. She seemed to sense Julie's arrival because she opened her eyes.

'My dear, I'm sorry you had to cut your trip short to come

and see a dying lady.' But despite the words, Julie could see the relief in the faded blue eyes.

'If you think that any trip is more important than being with an old friend when she needs me, then you don't know me very well, Lexy Dunlop,' Julie scolded, although her heart was breaking. She could see the end was close.

'How was it? Did you find what you were looking for?' For a moment Julie wondered if her friend was confused. But then as Lexy gave her a weak smile she realised that the old lady meant exactly what she'd said.

'Yes, I did. I found everything I ever wanted,' she said softly. 'How did you know?'

'Because I know you, my dear. Something has changed you. And I know if you let any man get to know you—really know you—he'd never be able to resist you.'

'I love him, Lexy. And he loves me. He wants us to get married.'

'I'm so happy for you. Now I know you are happy, I can go.'

'Please, Lexy, I still need you. Who else am I going to confide in?' Julie felt her throat tighten. She wasn't ready to lose another person she loved.

'Oh, you don't need me any more.' Julie had to strain to catch the words. 'You have Kim and now your doctor. It's him you need to confide in.' Lexy closed her eyes and as her breathing deepened, Julie realised she had fallen asleep.

As she sat by the bed in the soft glow from the bedside, holding her old friend's hand, gently stroking the paper-thin skin, Julie fought back tears. It was typical of life, she thought, to give with one hand while taking away with the other.

She stayed by Lexy's side through the night. At times her friend came round and mumbled a few words that Julie couldn't follow but which seemed to relate to her past life. She whispered her dead husband's name. Just before dawn, Lexy opened her eyes.

'Promise me,' she whispered

'Anything,' Julie replied.

'Promise me you'll always trust your heart. Promise me you'll never again hide from life—no matter what.' Eyes the colour of a cloudless sky burned into Julie's.

'I promise, Lexy. Just go to sleep now,' Julie said soothingly.

Julie watched as her friend breathed her last a few minutes later. There wasn't any point in calling the nurses. There was nothing anyone could do. Despite her grief, Julie knew that Lexy had had a good and full life. If she herself lived her life even half as fully as her old friend then she'd be happy.

Eventually having said her final goodbyes, and after letting the nurses know she'd be responsible for the funeral arrangements—there being no one else—Julie left the hospice.

Outside she switched her mobile back on. It was against hospice policy to leave it on inside the wards. There were no messages. Not even one from Pierre. Tired and distressed, she felt the tears well in her eyes. Then, hearing someone call her name, she looked up and there he was—standing in front of her. He held out his arms and wordlessly she stepped into them, resting her head against his chest.

'She is gone, your friend?' he said gently.

She nodded and then tears came in earnest. Soon she was sobbing, deep, racking sobs that came from the depths of her soul. It was as if the grief and hurt of all the years that she had suppressed was exploding from her heart. The hurt of her career cut short, Luke's betrayal, her mother's illness and death, her father's sudden death. It was all there.

Pierre held her, murmuring words in French, kissing the tears from her eyes. Then he picked her up tenderly and carried her over to the car. He sat her in the passenger seat, before climbing in and driving off. The tears were still flowing as they pulled up in front of Caroline's house. He came round to her side of the car and once again picked her up, and just as he had done in France—had it only been twenty-four hours ago?—carried her past an astonished-looking Caroline and upstairs into a bedroom. He laid her on the bed, gently removing her shoes. Then he lay down beside her and pulled her into his arms. Julie didn't know how long they lay like that. Her crying, him stroking her, making soothing noises. Eventually the storm of tears passed and she was able to speak.

'You came,' she hiccuped. 'I needed you and you came. Thank you.'

'Isn't that what husbands do for wives?' he said. 'Even before they are married? Don't they come to the other when the other is in need?'

'How did you get here?' she said. 'I thought there was only one flight a day?'

'I have my own plane. I keep it at the vineyard. I have been flying for years. Just like Jacques. We both had our pilot's licences. I thought Caroline would be too scared to come with me, but she insisted. She said you had looked after her, and she wasn't going to let the fact she was even more terri-fied of small planes than commercial aircraft stop her.'

'She's a brave girl.' Julie sniffed, touched that the girl had made the effort. She knew how much it must have cost her.

'She has learned to be brave from you,' Pierre said. 'You are a good teacher.'

'How is Alain?' Julie asked, snuggling into Pierre's arms.

'He is doing well. I am hopeful that he will regain almost full use of his hand in time. But we want him to stay in hospital for another day or two so I am sorry, *petite*, but I need to go back to oversee the vineyard until he leaves hospital. You can come with me.'

'Oh,' Julie said in a small voice, desperately disappointed. But she would have the rest of her life to be with him. She understood that in the meantime he had other responsibilities. But she had hoped he would be with her at Lexy's funeral.

'I can't come back. Not with the funeral to arrange. Besides, I am due back at work soon.'

'Don't worry about work. I will tell them you will be off for a few days, even a week.'

Julie sat up in bed. 'No, you won't.' she said firmly. 'I agreed to marry you, not let you run my life. If I don't go to work some other junior will have to cover my shift and it's just not fair. Anyway,' she said, her voice cracking a little, 'I have to be here to organise the funeral and I will need a day off to attend it and they'll have to cover for me then.'

'Okay. I will not interfere. But could you stay here with Caroline until I get back? I would be happier if I knew you were together.'

'I think it might be difficult for her, going through funeral arrangements so soon… But if she wants me to stay with her, of course I will.'

Pierre was drawing her towards him but, suddenly aware that she must look a fright, Julie got out of bed and stood. 'I need to wash my face. Then I think we should speak to Caroline. Have you told her our news?'

'I told her on the plane over here. Naturally she is delighted. She says there isn't anyone else she'd like better for an aunt. She wants to help plan the wedding, but I told her it will be a small affair and that we both want it to happen soon.' While he was talking Pierre had also got to his feet. Julie looked at him, puzzled.

'Doesn't the bride get a say in the when and where of her wedding?' she asked.

'Of course. I just thought you would like a small wedding since neither of us have much family. And I don't see any reason to delay, do you? I want to be married as soon as possible. I thought you did, too.'

He came up behind her and circled her waist with his arms, pulling her against his chest. 'I want to make an honest woman of you,' he whispered into her hair. She relaxed into him for a moment. It was good that he wanted them to be married soon, wasn't it? Why then did she feel that small flicker of doubt?

CHAPTER NINE

JULIE said goodbye to Pierre a couple of hours later. Although she knew it would only be a few days before she saw him again, she couldn't help the uneasy feeling she still had. Probably down to Lexy's death, she tried to reassure herself. That and the fact most women weren't separated from their fiancés so soon after getting engaged. Once he was back and they had a chance to make proper plans, she'd feel better. She wondered if the feeling of uncertainty was down to not quite being able to make herself believe that Pierre loved her and wanted to marry her. Of all the women in the world he wanted her. But then the feeling of disquiet was back. He hadn't actually told her that he loved her, had he? And hadn't he tried to warn her off, saying he would always love Iona? She shook her head to banish the thoughts. These were the imaginings of the old under-confident Julie—not the woman she was now. Of course Pierre loved her. He wanted to marry her after all, and he had flown all the way from France just to be with her for a few hours when she needed him most.

Caroline had expressed her delight and whole-hearted approval of the upcoming marriage. 'I just knew that you'd be perfect for each other,' she said. She had told Julie that she'd like it if she could stay, although Julie suspected she was only saying that because Pierre didn't want Julie to be on her own. Whatever the reason, it made little difference to Julie where she stayed. All she wanted was to get through the funeral.

She went back to work a few days later, spending the time before the funeral assisting one of the other surgeons in Theatre. Although he was an excellent surgeon, he didn't have Pierre's deft touch, Julie thought. She couldn't put her finger on it but there was something that made Pierre stand out from any other surgeon that Julie had worked with. It wasn't just because she was in love with him, she had recognised that something from the minute she had watched him operate. She missed Pierre, but her work and making the arrangements for Lexy's funeral left little time for brooding. In the evenings Caroline and Julie shared supper that Caroline prepared then the teenager would go and see her friends for a couple of hours. Pierre phoned to say he'd be back the day after the funeral. He told her that he wanted to be with her, to support her, but he was still needed in France. He said he was missing her, longing to see her, but still he didn't tell her he loved her. After he spoke to her he would have a few words with Caroline. Julie was able to reassure him that these days his niece seemed more settled and although still sad at times appeared to be coming to terms with her parents' death. Apart from Caroline, there was no one else Julie could share her news with. Kim was still on holiday with her husband, and although they had spoken on the phone, Julie wanted to tell her her news in person. Whenever someone mentioned Pierre's name at the hospital, she shivered with delight. How astonished they would all be when they heard that they were to be married.

The day of the funeral arrived. It was to be a small affair with only Julie, Caroline and some of the nurses from the hospital there to see Lexy on to her final journey. There was no one else, Lexy's husband and friends all having passed way before the old lady.

Clouds hung in an ominous sky as Julie stood with Caroline next to her by the side of the grave. The ceremony at the church had been a brief but moving affair and as she watched the coffin being lowered into the grave, Julie felt her throat close.

She whispered her goodbyes as she and Caroline turned away. Caroline held onto Julie's arm as if to reassure her. They returned to Julie's flat so that Julie could pick up some fresh clothes. Caroline put on the gas fire to warm the flat while Julie gathered some clothes together.

'Uncle Pierre is coming back tomorrow,' Caroline said. 'I bet you'll be glad to see him.'

Julie smiled. 'I can't wait,' she admitted.

'Then can we start planning the wedding?' Caroline said excitedly.

'Of course,' Julie said. 'You know I want you to be my bridesmaid, along with my friend Kim.'

'Just as long as you don't make me wear some pink, fluffy creation- then I'd be honoured,' Caroline said with a small bow.

'Don't worry you won't have to wear pink!' Julie laughed.

'I think it's great that you and Pierre are going to live in France,' Caroline continued. 'And I have decided to continue my studies in France after the summer, so we'll all be together.'

Julie frowned. 'Pierre and I haven't discussed where we're going to live after we get married,' she said. 'I'm not sure I want to leave Scotland.'

Caroline looked puzzled. 'He sounded as if it's all decided. He said there was too much to remind us of Mama and Papa here. He said we will never forget them, but we should start somewhere afresh.'

Julie felt her blood run cold. 'What else did he say?' she said grimly.

'Only that he promised he would always love Mama, and I wasn't to think he was forgetting about her. He said the three of us would be a new family.'

So he was still in love with Iona. Of course he was. She was such a fool. He'd never said otherwise. Why had she ever thought that she could compete with a dead woman's memory? How could she have been so stupid to believe even for one moment that he had fallen in love with *her*? But, she reminded herself, he had never actually said he loved her— not once. Had he thought that she was so lonely, so desperate that she would fall into his arms, only too grateful that someone like him wanted to marry someone like her? And this way he could keep his promise to Iona. He would look after her daughter while not betraying her memory by marrying someone he loved. How could she have let herself believe that Pierre loved *her*? After all, he had tried to warn her he could never love another.

Caroline had stopped talking. She looked at Julie and then covered her mouth with her hand.

'I'm sorry, Julie. That was a dumb thing to say. He loves you now. He must do. You are so fantastic. Now I've gone and spoiled everything. I shouldn't have told you what he said. Somehow it came out all wrong. Not the way he explained it at all.'

Julie hugged the distraught girl. 'You were right to tell me,' she said. 'Pierre should have told me himself.'

'He'll be back tomorrow,' Caroline said desperately. 'He can convince you himself then. Please, in the meantime, forget I ever opened my mouth.'

'Its okay, Caroline. Whatever you told me was only the truth. I should have guessed there was another reason for him wanting to marry me. But I don't think we'll be getting married after all.'

It was a subdued evening for the two women. Julie let her mobile ring when she saw Pierre's number on the screen, and she made Caroline tell Pierre she was in the bath when he tried the landline.

She barely slept that night, wondering what she should do. The thought of facing Pierre was unbearable. Happily it was Saturday and she wasn't expected at work. Making up her mind, she threw a few clothes into a bag and, leaving Caroline a note telling her not to worry, that she was going away for a couple of days, she drove to her flat. There she collected her skis and boots. As always, when life got her down, Julie headed for the mountains. Thankfully, although it was the beginning of April, there was still snow in the Cairngorms. She would stay in her usual bed and breakfast while she worked out what to do. She had left a note for Pierre, explaining that she'd had second thoughts about wedding and needed time on her own to think. He wasn't to come looking for her and if he cared about her at all, he would grant her this time on her own.

Soon, just had the sun had fully risen in the sky she was on the road, heading north. As she drove, she kept going over everything in her head. Admittedly she had almost flung herself at Pierre. She recoiled, recalling how she had responded to his kisses. No wonder he thought her a solution to his problems. No doubt he saw how love-struck she was.

Too smitten to ask questions. Too much in love to demand that her wishes were taken into account. He probably thought of her as someone who he could live with, someone who could give him children and be satisfied with whatever scraps of affection he threw her way. She shook her head to clear it. But the way he had held her, the way he had comforted her outside the hospice. Surely these were the actions of a man who cared? But in her soul she knew she wasn't really in a position to judge. She had so little experience of men or relationships. He, on the other hand, had so much.

By lunchtime she had booked in with a surprised but welcoming Doris and was on the top of the mountain. The snow was melting, and had almost completed disappeared at the lower levels. There had been avalanche warnings posted at the bottom of the lifts, and Julie knew better than to venture off piste where the danger was. Nevertheless, she carried her emergency backpack with her. It was force of habit. She looked across the Grey Corries to the Mamores in the distance and down into Five Finger Gully. Although it was the most challenging run on the mountain, it was child's play to Julie. Besides, she wanted to ski the most difficult run she could. She wanted to lose herself in the speed and concentration she needed to descend in the quickest possible time. Her record was under five minutes. Today she wanted to cut at least thirty seconds off that. She needed to remind herself that there was one area where she was better than everyone else. She needed to regain her self-esteem, which had been so cruelly torn away from her.

There was hardly anyone else on the slopes despite it being the weekend. It was now the end of the season, and only the hardiest skiers would be on the slopes; the beginners and less

experienced put off by the conditions and the threat of ava-
lanches. The sun was losing its heat as the clouds covered the
sky. Up at the top of the mountain the wind was strong,
whipping snow around Julie's head. Not for the first time she
was glad of her goggles. Apart from protecting her eyes from
the stinging snow, they gave her sight a depth she needed in
what could very quickly become a white-out.

She skied down the run, letting the exhilaration of the
speed whip away all thoughts of Pierre and his deceit. At the
bottom she checked her watch. Five minutes exactly. Too
slow. She would repeat the run until she was able to cut at least
thirty seconds off that time. It might take her the rest of the
afternoon, but it would have the added bonus of exhausting
her. Hopefully she'd sleep tonight. She had spent too many
nights tossing and turning lately. She took the lift back to the
top and prepared for another descent. Before she could set off,
however, she felt her arm pulled in a vice-like grip. Spinning
round, she came face to face with Pierre. Even in the swirling
snow, she could tell he was angry. His eyes glinted.

'I knew I would find you here,' he said grimly.

'I thought I asked you not to come looking for me,' she bit
back, furious. Why couldn't he leave her alone? Allow her to
salvage even the smallest vestige of pride?

'We can't talk here,' he said, raising his voice to compete
with the sound of the wind. 'Let's go down and find somewhere out of this crazy weather.'

Julie laughed bitterly. 'You can do as you please, but for
now I'm skiing.' Twisting out of his grasp, she turned and
headed down the slope. She was conscious of him following
her, but she increased her speed, putting more distance
between them. She didn't want to talk to him. Not now. Not

ever. At least not until she had calmed down—possibly in a hundred years' time. If then.

But as she came to the first sharp corner she noticed a couple of skiers below her. The figures, a man and a woman from the shape and size of them, looked to be out of control. By this time visibility was almost non-existent and Julie could tell that they had no idea that they were heading for a steep verge, which, even supposing they managed to negotiate it safely, would take them off piste into the avalanche danger zone. The smaller of the figures, wearing a red all-in-one skisuit, was leading the way, with the larger skier, in black, following close behind. Julie knew that there was no point in calling out. The snow would muffle her voice—there was no chance they would hear her in time. She knew there was only one viable option—she had to stop them before they reached the edge. Without breaking speed, she headed off after them.

Within seconds she had almost caught up with the skiers. She wasn't quite sure how she would stop them, she only knew she had to get to them before it was too late.

She came up alongside the red-suited skier, slowed down and pointed frantically away from the cliff edge. For a moment she caught a glimpse of frightened eyes, then, realising the skier hadn't the control to remove herself from danger, Julie leant her body into hers, forcing her skis in the opposite direction from the cliff. And then the inevitable happened. Their skis caught, catapulting them both down the slope.

Julie had fallen enough times to know to relax and let her body go. She would come to a halt eventually. In what seemed like minutes, but could only have been a seconds, she slid to a stop. The red-suited blonde, minus both skis, was lying in a crumpled heap several metres ahead of Julie.

Julie glanced around. The other skier, oblivious to what had happened behind him, was still heading for the verge. Julie hesitated for a moment, torn between helping the injured skier or going after the man. But just at that moment Pierre arrived.

'Are you all right?' he asked Julie, anxiously scanning her body for evidence of injury. At Julie's nod, he seemed to relax slightly. '*Dieu*, for a minute I thought you were going to kill yourself! We will speak about it later.' Then he was on his knees by the injured skier.

Knowing that the injured woman would be well cared for, Julie turned her skis back towards where she had seen the man disappear. The snow away from the run was deep and it was unlikely he would be badly injured. Nevertheless, she needed to make sure. She had to walk back up the slope before she could gain enough height to ski towards him. Happily the snow had stopped, but even so, with the rise in the verge blocking her view, the other skier was out of her sight. Once Julie had gained enough height she skied towards the edge, stopping at the cusp of the slope. Below her, about fifty metres away, was the body of the man. She could see that he wasn't hurt badly as he was struggling to extricate himself from a deep mound of snow. She was about to turn back to the injured woman when a crack like the sound of a cannon going off boomed across the snow. Turning towards the sound, she was horrified to see a lump of snow break off from the top of the mountain above the struggling skier and begin to make its way down the slope, increasing in size and momentum as she watched. Knowing that she was witnessing the beginning of an avalanche, and that the black-suited skier was directly in its path, she made up her mind. By this time he had got to his feet and was

looking behind him. He seemed incapable of moving out of
the way. Julie guessed she had thirty seconds—maybe less—
in which to act.

'Julie! No!' Pierre shouted from behind her. Somehow he
must have guessed what she was thinking. For a split second
she held his gaze, committing his dear face to her heart. She
smiled briefly, before heading off towards the man. There was
a faint chance that she would get to him in time to lead him
out of the path of the avalanche. If not, well, she wouldn't
think about the if not. It wasn't that she wanted to put herself
in danger, and she certainly didn't want to die, but she couldn't
just stand watching while a man was killed in front of her.

As she shot towards him, she glanced to her left. Coming
towards her was a wall of snow, almost of tidal wave size and
intensity. If the skier in front of her was capable of movement,
there was still a chance he could ski out of its path. But he
seemed rooted to the spot. Now she had no option. She stopped
in front of him, knowing they had seconds before they were
hit by the avalanche. With a strength born of desperation, she
pushed him down into the snow. Then, throwing herself on top
of him and in the last second before they were submerged, she
cupped her hands in front of her mouth to create an air pocket.
Then the snow hit and everything went dark.

Pierre watched in horror as the cascading snow hit Julie and
her companion, covering them completely before continuing
down the slope. 'No!' he cried out into the silent snow-covered
mountains. In the distance he heard the mournful wail of the
klaxon that would alert the rescue services to the avalanche.
They were a regular occurrence in France and Pierre knew
only too well that often lives were lost, either through the

sheer impact of the snow or, if they survived that, a lack of oxygen. He also knew that there was a window of about fifteen minutes if the victims were to be found alive. After that their chances diminished with every passing second. If they weren't found and dug out within the first thirty minutes, the chances of survival were almost non-existent.

'Julie. My Julie. *Qu'est que tu as fait?* What have you done? And I didn't even get the chance to tell you I loved you,' he shouted, but the wind whipped away his words. She had to know. If she was dead, that would break him in two, but if she died believing that he didn't love her… He dismissed the thought. That wasn't going to let that happen—he wouldn't let it happen. He hadn't found her after all these years only to lose her now.

The woman at his feet had nothing worse than a badly sprained ankle and was shocked and frightened. But he had to leave her. He had to find Julie. He would dig her out with his bare hands if he had to!

He told the frightened woman to stay where she was until help came. He instructed her to keep trying her mobile, although he knew it was unlikely she would get a signal. Then he sped towards where he had last seen Julie and the black-suited skier.

He could only guess where they might be buried. It was possible that the weight of the snow had dragged them much further down the slope, but he had to start somewhere.

He looked at his watch, amazed to find only a minute had passed since the snow had covered the two bodies. Refusing to let himself think about the possibility of Julie not being alive, he called out her name before dropping to his knees and frantically tearing at the snow.

* * *

Julie couldn't hear or see anything. She took stock of her situation. Her body was pinned by the weight of the snow, but she was aware of the body of the skier under her arm.

She was able to twist her head just enough to see that she had she managed to create a small but potential lifesaving pocket of air. Spitting snow from her mouth, she called to the still figure next to her.

'Hey, mister. Are you okay?' There was no reply. He was either unconscious or, worse, dead. She tried to move her arm. It took great deal of effort, but finally she was able to release it from the snow. She felt along the figure until eventually she could feel the top of his jacket and the cold flesh of his neck. Straining to reach around the side of his neck, she eventually found the carotid pulse. A regular pressure underneath her fingertips told her he was alive. She closed her eyes. Thank God. She fought against rising panic. Take one step at a time, she told herself. You have air—not a lot, admittedly, but enough to buy some time. Pierre would find her. They were alive and they would be rescued—she had to hang into the thought.

She let her thoughts turn to Pierre. What would he be thinking up there? Probably that she was dead. He had no way of knowing that the force of the snow hadn't killed her outright. She wondered what he would be going through. She had been involved in rescues like this one before and she knew the desperate race against time that everyone looking for her would be feeling. Please, God, let them find us in time.

Pierre was also praying as he dug frantically with his hands, knowing all the while that it was no use. He needed a pole to try and locate them and a shovel to dig them out, and he had neither. But he couldn't just sit back and do nothing, even though he could see a rescue team in the distance. 'Hurry up!' he shouted, looking at his watch. Ten minutes had passed. If she wasn't already dead, her chances of survival would be diminishing with every minute. Then he had an idea. Grabbing his ski pole, he pulled the bit off the end. Now he at least had something with which to probe beneath the snow. Steadying the panic that threatened to drive him mad, he set about methodically testing the snow for her body.

Why hadn't he told her he loved her when he'd had the chance? If he had told her, she would never have believed he was marrying her out of some mistaken loyalty to Iona. He had thought his feelings for her were perfectly obvious. But he should have thought about Julie's fragile self-esteem. Her lack of belief that anyone could love her. She just didn't see herself the way others did. Beautiful, fiery, loving and loyal. Who could not love her? And he did. More than life. More even than he had ever loved Iona. This time he loved completely and with no doubt. Julie was the woman he wanted to have his children, the woman he wanted by his side every day of his life, the woman he wanted to grow old with. He groaned aloud. He couldn't bear it if he had lost her. Not when he had so recently discovered her. Not when there was still so much to learn about each other and he had thought they'd have a lifetime to learn it.

The rescue team had arrived and were pulling out their equipment, getting ready for the search. One of them was attending to the injured skier Pierre had had to abandon. The rest were pulling out poles and shovels.

'How many? Where?' the rescuer in charge asked.

Pierre pointed to where he had last seen Julie and her companion. Although he wanted nothing more than to grab a shovel from the man's hands and dig until he found Julie, he knew that it wasn't the best way to make sure they found her alive.

'Hey, over here!' one of the men shouted, standing over a piece of ground only a metre or two away from where Julie had flung herself down, and from where Pierre had been searching. He felt the first real stirrings of hope. At least now they had a small chance of finding her alive. He looked at his watch. Fifteen minutes had passed. This time there was no stopping him as he joined the other men digging at the point where the signal had come from. A probe had told them that there were bodies submerged at that point and how far they could dig with the shovels before reverting to their hands.

As they dug frantically Pierre felt something beneath his hands. It was a body. Alive or dead, he had no way of knowing. Another minute passed until at last they a hand and then a black skisuit. It was the skier Julie had gone after. Pierre was torn between hope and despair. It wasn't Julie, but if they had found one of them, the other couldn't be far away.

'Hold on, Julie,' he yelled. 'Just another few minutes.' He had no way of knowing if she could hear him, but he had to believe she was alive. As they pulled the man out Pierre could tell instantly that he was unconscious, perhaps dead. Dread washed over him, turning his blood cold. If he was dead, then it was likely that Julie was too. He carried on digging. And then suddenly he felt something solid beneath his fingers. It had to be her. Scraping away the snow, quickly but gently he exposed her face. It was deathly pale, the colour of the washed-out sky, her lips tinged with blue. Others were helping him, clearing away the snow until at last they were able to pull her free. For a moment his heart stopped. Were they too late?

As they laid her gently on the ground, he felt for a pulse. Yes, underneath his frozen fingers he could feel its shallow beat. Calling for an oxygen mask, he placed it over her lips. Then he pulled her body into his as if he could transfer his life force into her. She shuddered in his arms and then coughed weakly. He lifted his head to look at her dear, precious features. Her lips were moving. He thought she was trying to say his name.

With a cry of triumph he pulled her back into his arms, calling her name over and over. He could feel her breath against his cheek. He looked into her face, her dearly beloved face. Her eyes flickered open. 'Pierre,' she said. 'You found me!' And then as he felt his eyes burn with relief she smiled faintly and closed her eyes once more.

Julie came to in a hospital bed. She had been vaguely aware of gentle arms lifting her onto a stretcher and taking her off the mountain. She remembered Pierre being there, his eyes dark with fear, him calling her name, telling her he loved her over and over. She had tried to tell him that it was all right, that he didn't have to pretend any more, but she hadn't been able to form the words through her frozen lips.

She focussed on her surroundings. Her body felt as if she had been run over by a car, but apart from that she seemed, miraculously, to have escaped serious injury.

A shape leaned over her. Pierre, unshaven and the most dishevelled she had ever seen him, brushed a stray lock of hair from her eyes. Despite his appearance, he had never seemed more dear to her.

'You are okay,' he said hoarsely. 'You are a very lucky woman.'

Then it all came rushing back to her. Caroline explaining

that Pierre still loved his dead sister-in law. That he only wanted *her* to marry him so she would come and live in France.

'You don't have to stay,' she said. Even in her fatigue she was conscious of the need to salvage some pride. 'I'm all right—you said so yourself.'

'What were you doing back there?' he said. Now he seemed angry with her.

'I couldn't leave him,' she said. 'Is he okay?'

'He's fine. So is the woman he was with. But you! Why do you always put your life at risk for others? Don't you care about living?' He said that as if the words had been torn from somewhere deep inside him.

Julie struggled to sit up. Lying down in the hospital bed, she felt at too much of a disadvantage. Seeing her struggle, Pierre helped her up, arranging the pillows behind her back.

'Don't be silly,' she said crossly. 'I want to live as much as the next person. But sometimes in life we have to put others first.' Not that he'd know anything about *that*, she reminded herself. He was the kind of man who used people to get what he wanted. He wouldn't understand.

Pierre slipped an arm around her shoulder and pulled her into his chest. She could feel the beat of his heart through the thin material of his sweater and smell the faint citrus tang of his aftershave. She felt a wave of grief wash over her. This would be the last time she would find herself in his arms.

'Why did you run away from me?' His voice was deep with emotion, the French accent more pronounced than ever. Julie closed her eyes against the pain in her heart. More than anything she wanted him to leave so that she could nurse her aching heart away from his searching eyes.

'Caroline told me what you said about Iona. That you

couldn't bear to go on living in Scotland,' she said. 'It explains why you asked me to marry you.'

'You think I asked you to marry me because I wanted Iona's daughter to live with me?' He laughed but it was a mirthless sound. '*De bleu*, Julie. You must have a very bad opinion of me.'

'But it's true, isn't it? Caroline wouldn't lie to me.'

Pierre sighed and rested his chin on the top of her head. His hand caressed the side of her jaw. It was as if he needed to reassure himself she was still in one piece.

'It's only partly true. I do want you to come and live with me in France. And if that helps Caroline, it would make me very happy. I feel I would have paid back some of the debt I owe my brother, and Iona, by making a home for their child. But if that is not what you want, then I will be wherever you are.'

Pierre tipped Julie's chin so she was looking into his eyes. What she saw there made her shiver with hope.

'You are all that matters to me,' he said firmly. 'When I thought I had lost you, I knew my life was over. Without you there is nothing for me. I love you. It is you I want. No one and nothing else matters.'

'Are you sure?' Julie breathed, feeling a burst of sunshine permeate her soul. 'Because I would rather be alone than be married to a man who doesn't love me properly.'

Pierre cursed in fast-flowing, incomprehensible French.

'I see,' he said, 'that I am going to have to spend the rest of my life convincing you of how much I love you. It doesn't matter how long it takes—I can wait. But one day—soon, I hope—you will learn to believe me. Then we will be married.' He kissed her lips softly. 'But don't make me wait too long. Please.'

'Well, Dr Favatier.' Julie returned his kisses, knowing that this time she had found someone who would love her the way she had always dreamt of. 'You'd better start persuading me.'

A few weeks later, Julie stood beside Caroline and Pierre at the side of Jacques and Iona's gravestones. Spring had come in earnest and the cemetery was blanketed with tulips. The smell of honeysuckle drifted in the warm breeze. Birds called to each other over the sound of distant traffic.

Caroline tucked her arm in Julie's, and sniffed. 'It is so peaceful here.' The young girl knelt and laid flowers on her parents' grave. '*Bonne nuit*, Mama and Papa. You can sleep peacefully now. I'm going to be all right.' She stood and, linking her arm in Pierre's, started to walk towards the car. 'Are you coming, Julie?' Pierre called to her. 'Our guests are waiting for us.'

Julie looked at him, so handsome in his morning suit. He was her husband, and she could still hardly believe it. Her wedding dress fluttered in the breeze.

'You go ahead, I won't be a moment.' Crouching by the side of the graves, she laid her wedding bouquet on top of Iona's.

'Your daughter is a fine young woman,' she whispered, blinking away a tear. 'Pierre and I will watch over her as if she were our own.' She pressed her hand to her belly. There was no sign of her pregnancy yet, but she was sure she could feel the tiny life growing inside her. 'Pierre, Caroline, this little baby will all be a family. We'll come and see you often, I promise.' She stood and looked towards where her husband and niece were waiting for her. Her heart sang as she took in their beloved figures. Life could be perfect after all.

MILLS & BOON
MEDICAL
On sale 3rd July 2009

SURGEON BOSS, BACHELOR DAD
by Lucy Clark

Agreeing to a date with a handsome stranger is totally
out of character for Megan Edwards, and she is horrified
when her date turns out to be her new colleague, surgeon
Loughlin McCloud! Romance isn't on Megan's agenda –
but this single dad and his daughter have found Megan
creeping into their dreams of a happy family…

THE GREEK DOCTOR'S PROPOSAL
by Molly Evans

Jeannine Carlyle left the ER because she needed time to
heal from her devastating break-up. But her new boss,
Dr Miklo Kyriakides, sends her emotions and body into
freefall! Miklo must make Jeannine realise that the key to
her happiness lies in them being together, for good!

SINGLE FATHER: WIFE AND MOTHER WANTED
by Sharon Archer

Having captured the hearts of dedicated – and *gorgeous* –
GP Matt Gardiner and his young son, Caitlin Butler-Brown
longs to become part of their family permanently. But she
has a secret – one that could change everything…

In the Sheikh's power

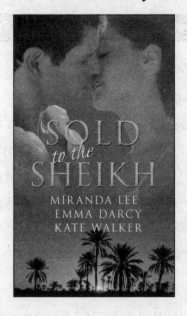

Be tempted by three seductive Sheikhs in:

Love-Slave to the Sheikh by Miranda Lee
Traded to the Sheikh by Emma Darcy
At the Sheikh's Command by Kate Walker

Available 5th June 2009

www.millsandboon.co.uk

FREE!

2 Books
and a surprise gift!

We would like to take this opportunity to thank you for reading this Mills & Boon® book by offering you the chance to take TWO more specially selected titles from the Medical™ series absolutely FREE! We're also making this offer to introduce you to the benefits of the Mills & Boon® Book Club™—

- ★ **FREE home delivery**
- ★ **FREE gifts and competitions**
- ★ **FREE monthly Newsletter**
- ★ **Exclusive Mills & Boon Book Club offers**
- ★ **Books available before they're in the shops**

Accepting these FREE books and gift places you under no obligation to buy, you may cancel at any time, even after receiving your free shipment. Simply complete your details below and return the entire page to the address below. You don't even need a stamp!

YES! Please send me 2 free Medical books and a surprise gift. I understand that unless you hear from me, I will receive 4 superb new titles every month for just £2.99 each, postage and packing free. I am under no obligation to purchase any books and may cancel my subscription at any time. The free books and gift will be mine to keep in any case.

M9ZEF

Ms/Mrs/Miss/Mr ....Initials ....
BLOCK CAPITALS PLEASE
Surname...
Address..

....
....Postcode ....

Send this whole page to:
UK: FREEPOST CN81, Croydon, CR9 3WZ